ANGELICA'S SMILE

Andrea Camilleri is one of Italy's most famous contemporary writers. His Montalbano series has been adapted for Italian television and translated into several languages. He lives in Rome.

Stephen Sartarelli is an award-winning translator. He is also the author of three books of poetry, most recently *The Open Vault*. He lives in France.

Also by Andrea Camilleri

ANDREA CAMILLERI

ANGELICA'S SMILE

Translated by Stephen Sartarelli

MANTLE

First published 2013 by Penguin Books,
a member of Penguin Group (USA) Inc., New York

First published in the UK 2014 by Mantle
an imprint of Pan Macmillan, a division of Macmillan Publishers Limited
Pan Macmillan, 20 New Wharf Road, London N1 9RR
Basingstoke and Oxford
Associated companies throughout the world
www.panmacmillan.com

ISBN 978-1-4472-4913-9

Copyright © Sellerio Editore 2010
Translation copyright © Stephen Sartarelli 2013

Originally published in Italian 2011 as *Il sorriso di Angelica* by Sellerio Editore, Palermo.

The right of Andrea Camilleri to be identified as the
author of this work has been asserted by him in accordance
with the Copyright, Designs and Patents Act 1988.

3 5 7 9 8 6 4

A CIP catalogue record for this book is available from the British Library.

Typeset by Ellipsis Digital Limited, Glasgow
Printed and bound by CPI Group (UK) Ltd, Croydon, CR0 4YY

Visit **www.panmacmillan.com** to read more about all our books
and to buy them. You will also find features, author interviews and
news of any author events, and you can sign up for e-newsletters
so that you're always first to hear about our new releases.

ANGELICA'S SMILE

ONE

He awoke with a start and sat up in bed, eyes already open. He was sure he'd heard someone talking in his bedroom. And since he was alone in the house, he was alarmed.

Then he started laughing, having remembered that Livia had arrived unannounced at his place that evening. The surprise visit had pleased him immensely, at least at first. And there she was now, sleeping soundly beside him.

A still-violet shaft of the dawn's very earliest light shone through the shutter. He let his eyelids droop without bothering to look at the clock, in hopes of getting a few more hours of sleep.

But then his eyes suddenly popped open again. Something had just occurred to him.

If someone had spoken in his bedroom, it could only have been Livia. She had therefore been talking in her sleep. But this had never happened before. Or perhaps it wasn't the first time. But if she had in fact talked in her sleep before, she'd done it so quietly that it hadn't woken him.

And it was possible she was, at that moment, still in the same dream state and might say a few more words.

So this was an opportunity not to be missed.

People who suddenly start talking in their sleep can't help but say true things, the truths that they have inside them. He remembered reading that it was impossible to tell lies or stretch the truth in a dream state, because one is defenceless when asleep, as helpless and innocent as a baby.

It was very important not to miss anything Livia said. Important for two reasons. The first was general in nature, being that a man can live a hundred years at a woman's side, sleep with her, have children with her, breathe the same air as her, and think he knows her as well as humanly possible, and still, in the end, feel as though he never really knows what she is like deep inside.

The other reason was more specific and immediate.

He carefully got out of bed and went and looked through the slats of the shutter. It promised to be a lovely day, without clouds or wind.

Then he went over to Livia's side of the bed, pulled up a chair, and sat down at the head, as in an all-night vigil at the hospital.

The previous evening – and this was the more specific

reason – Livia had made a huge fuss in a fit of jealousy, ruining the pleasure of her surprise visit.

Things had gone as follows.

The telephone had rung and she went to answer.

But as soon as she said hello, a woman's voice at the other end said: 'Oh, I'm sorry, I must have the wrong number.' And promptly hung up.

And so Livia got it in her head that the caller was a woman he was having an affair with, that they'd arranged to meet that evening, and that when she'd heard Livia's voice she'd hung up.

'I guess I rained on your parade, eh? . . . When the cat's away, the mice will play! . . . Out of sight, out of mind! . . .'

There was no making her see reason, and things ended terribly because Montalbano had reacted badly, disgusted not so much by Livia's suspicions as by the endless barrage of clichés she fired at him.

So now Montalbano was hoping that Livia would say something stupid in her sleep, anything that might give him ammunition for a proper revenge.

He suddenly had a great desire to smoke a cigarette, but restrained himself – first, because if Livia woke up and found him smoking in the bedroom, a revolution might break out, and second, because the smoke itself might wake her up.

About two hours later, he got a cramp in his left calf.

To make it go away, he started swinging his leg back and forth and, as a result, ended up giving the wooden bed-frame a violent kick with his bare foot.

It hurt like hell, but he managed to hold back the avalanche of curses that threatened to burst out.

The kick had an effect, however, because Livia sighed, moved a little, and then spoke.

Giving first a little laugh, in a full voice with no trace of hoarseness, she said distinctly:

'No, Carlo, not from behind.'

Montalbano nearly fell out of his chair. This was a bit too much of a good thing, for Christ's sake!

A couple of muttered words would have sufficed, just enough for him to build a castle of baseless accusations, Jesuit-like.

But Livia had uttered a whole sentence, loud and clear! *Fuck!*

As if she had been wide awake.

And it was a sentence that suggested just about everything, even the worst.

She had never said a word to him about any Carlo. Why not?

If she'd never mentioned him, there must be a reason. And what exactly was it she didn't want Carlo to do to her from behind?

Did that mean: from in front, OK, but not from behind?

He broke into a cold sweat.

He was tempted to wake Livia up, shake her roughly and, glaring wild-eyed, ask her in an imperious, cop-like voice: 'Who is Carlo? Is he your lover?'

But she was a woman, after all.

And therefore likely to deny everything, even when groggy with sleep. No, that would be a wrong move.

It was best to summon the strength to wait a while and try to broach the subject at the right moment.

But when was the right moment?

Anyway, he would need to have a certain amount of time at his disposal, since it would be a mistake to bring the question up directly. Livia would immediately go on the defensive. No, he needed to take a roundabout approach, without arousing any suspicion.

He decided to go and have a shower.

Going back to bed was out of the question now.

✻

He was drinking his first coffee of the morning when the telephone rang.

It was eight o'clock. He wasn't in the mood to hear about any little murders. If anything, he might kill somebody himself instead, given half a chance.

Preferably someone by the name of Carlo.

He'd guessed right. It was Catarella.

'Ahh, Chief, Chief! Wha'z ya doin', sleepin'?'

'No, Cat, I was awake. What's up?'

'Wha'ss up is 'ere's a buggery tha'ss up.'

Montalbano hesitated. Then it dawned on him.

'A burglary, you mean? So why are you bothering *me*, then?'

'Chief, beckin' yer partin', bu—'

'But nothing! No beckons or partings! Phone Inspector Augello at once!'

Catarella was about to start crying.

''Ass jess what I wannit a say t'yiz, ya gotta 'scuse me, Chief. I wannit a say 'at Isspecter Augello was let go whereas of diss mornin'.'

Montalbano was stumped. You couldn't even sack your housekeeper these days!

'Let go? Who by?'

'Bu', Chief, i's youse yisself 'at let 'im go yisterday aftanoon!'

Montalbano remembered.

'Cat, he took a leave of absence, he wasn't let go!'

'Bu' ya gotta let 'im go f'r 'im to be assbent!'

'Listen, was Fazio let go too?'

''Ass also what I wannit a tell yiz. Dis mornin' 'ere's some trouble atta market an' so the afficer in quession izzatta scene o' the crime.'

It was hopeless. He would have to look into it himself. 'All right, is the aggrieved party there?'

Catarella paused for a moment before speaking. ''Ere meanin' where, Chief?'

'There, at the station, where else?'

'Chief, how's I asposta know 'oo this man is?'

'Is he there or isn't he?'

''Oo?'

'The aggrieved party.'

Catarella remained silent.

'Hello?'

Catarella didn't answer.

Montalbano thought the line had gone dead.

And he fell prey to that tremendous, cosmic, irrational fear that came over him whenever a phone call was cut off, as if he was the last person left alive in the universe.

He started shouting like a madman. 'Hello! Hello!'

'I'm right 'ere, Chief.'

'Why don't you answer?'

'Chief, promiss ya won' get upset if I tell yiz I dunno wha'ss a grieve party?'

Calm and patient, Montalbà, calm and patient. 'That'd be the person who got robbed, Cat.'

'Oh, that person! Bu' iss no party f'r 'im, Chief!'

'What's his name, Cat?'

''Is name's Piritone.'

Which in Sicilian means *big fart*. Was it possible?

'Are you sure that's his name?'

'Swear to God, Chief. Carlo Piritone.'

7

Montalbano felt like screaming. Two Carlos the same morning was too much to bear.

'Is Mr Piritone at the station?'

'Nah, Chief, 'e jess called. 'E lives a' Via Cavurro, nummer toitteen.'

'Ring him and tell him I'm on my way.'

Livia hadn't been woken up by either the phone or his yelling. In her sleep she had a faint smile on her lips.

Maybe she was still dreaming about Carlo. The bitch. He felt overwhelmed by uncontrollable rage. Grabbing a chair, he lifted it up and slammed it down on the floor.

Livia woke up suddenly, frightened. 'What was that?'

'Nothing, I'm sorry. I have to go out. I'll be back for lunch. *Ciao.*'

He ran out to avoid starting a fight.

*

Via Cavour was in the part of Vigàta where the rich people lived.

It had been designed by an architect who deserved a life sentence at the very least. One house looked like a Spanish galleon from the time of the pirates, while the one beside it was clearly inspired by the Pantheon in Rome . . .

Montalbano pulled up in front of number 13, which looked like the Pyramid of Menkaure, got out of the car, and went into the building. On the left was a little booth of wood and glass with the porter in it.

'Can you tell me what floor Mr Piritone lives on?'

The porter, a tall, burly man of about fifty who clearly spent a lot of time at the gym, put down the newspaper he was reading, took off his glasses, stood up, opened the door of the booth, and came out.

'No need to bother,' said Montalbano, 'all I need is—'

'All you need is for someone to smash your face in,' said the porter, raising a clenched fist.

Montalbano cringed and took a step back. What was his problem?

'Wait, listen, there must be some kind of misunderstanding. I'm looking for a Mr Piritone and I am—'

'You'd better make yourself scarce, and fast – I mean it.'

Montalbano lost patience. 'I'm Inspector Montalbano, damn it!'

The man looked surprised. 'Really?'

'Would you like to see my ID?'

The porter turned red in the face.

'Christ, it's true! Now I rec'nize ya! I'm sorry, I thought you were somebody tryin' t' fuck wit' me. I apologize, sir. But look, there's nobody here named Piritone.'

Naturally, Catarella, as usual, had given him the wrong name.

'Is there anyone with a similar name?'

'There's a Dr Peritore.'

'That could be him. What floor?'

'Second.'

The porter walked him to the lift, endlessly excusing himself and bowing.

It occurred to Montalbano that one of these days Catarella, by screwing up every name he gave him, was going to get him shot by someone who was a little on edge.

*

The slender, blond, well-dressed, bespectacled man of about forty who opened the door for the inspector was not as obnoxious as the inspector had hoped.

'Good morning, I'm Montalbano.'

'Please come in, Inspector, just follow me. I was fore-warned of your visit. Naturally the apartment is a mess; my wife and I didn't want to touch anything before you saw it.'

'You're right, I should have a look around.' Bedroom, dining room, guest room, living room, study, kitchen, and two bathrooms, all turned upside down.

Wardrobes and cabinets thrown open, contents scattered all over the floor, a bookcase completely emptied and the books strewn everywhere, desks and consoles with all their drawers open.

Policemen and burglars had one thing in common when searching somebody's home: an earthquake left things in better order.

In the kitchen was a young woman of about thirty, also blonde, pretty and polite.

'This is my wife, Caterina.'

'Would you like a coffee?' the woman asked.

'Sure, why not?' said the inspector.

After all, the kitchen was less topsy-turvy than any of the other rooms.

'Maybe it's best if we talk in here,' said Montalbano, sitting down in a chair.

Peritore did the same.

'The front door didn't look forced to me,' the inspector continued. 'Did they come in through the windows?'

'No, they just used our keys,' said Peritore.

He stuck a hand in his pocket, took out a set of keys, and put them on the table.

'They left them in the entrance hall.'

'I'm sorry. So you weren't home when the burglary occurred?'

'No. Last night we slept at our seaside house, at Punta Piccola.'

'Ah. And how did you get in if the burglars had your keys?'

'I always keep an extra set with the porter.'

'I'm sorry, I don't quite understand. So where did the burglars get the keys they used to enter your apartment?'

'From our seaside house.'

'While you were asleep?'

'Exactly.'

'And they didn't steal anything from that house?'

'They certainly did.'

'So in fact there were two burglaries?'

'That's right.'

'I beg your pardon, Inspector,' said Signora Caterina, pouring his coffee. 'Maybe it's better if I tell you. My husband is having trouble putting his thoughts in order. So. This morning we woke up around six, both of us with headaches. And we immediately realized that someone had broken in through the front door of our seaside home, knocked us out with some sort of gas, and had the run of the place.'

'You didn't hear anything?'

'Nothing at all.'

'Strange. Because, you see, they had to break through your front door before they could gas you. You just said so yourself. And so, you should have heard . . .'

'Well, we were . . .' The woman blushed.

'You were?'

'Let's say we were a bit tipsy. We were celebrating our fifth wedding anniversary.'

'I see.'

'I don't think we would even have heard a cannon go off.'

'Go on.'

'The burglars apparently found my husband's wallet in

his jacket, along with his ID card and our address – this one, I mean – as well as the keys to this place and to the car. So they quietly got into our car, came here, opened the door, stole what they wanted to steal, and went on their way.'

'What did they take?'

'Well, aside from the car, not very much from the seaside house, relatively speaking. Our wedding rings, my husband's Rolex, my diamond watch, a rather expensive necklace of mine, two thousand euros in cash, both of our computers, mobile phones, and our credit cards, which we immediately had cancelled.'

Not very much? If you say so.

'And a seascape by Carrà,' the lady concluded, cool as a cucumber.

Montalbano gave a start.

'A seascape by Carrà? And you had it out there, just like that?'

'Well, we were hoping no one would know how much it was worth.'

Whereas the burglars certainly did know how much it was worth.

'And what about here?'

'Here they made off with a lot more. For starters, my jewellery box with everything inside.'

'Valuable stuff?'

'About a million and a half euros.'

'What else?'

'My husband's four other Rolexes. He collects them.'

'And that's it?'

'Fifty thousand euros in cash. And . . .'

'And?'

'A Guttuso, a Morandi, a Donghi, a Mafai, and a Pirandello that my husband's father left to him in his will,' the woman said in a single breath.

In short, a whole gallery of art worth a fortune.

'One question,' said the inspector. 'Who knew that you were going to your house at Punta Piccola to celebrate your wedding anniversary?'

Husband and wife looked at each other for a moment. 'Well, our friends did,' the woman replied.

'How many friends do you mean?'

'About fifteen.'

'Do you have a housekeeper?'

'Yes.'

'Did she know too?'

'No.'

'Are you insured against burglary?'

'No.'

'Listen,' said Montalbano, standing up. 'You have to come to the station immediately and file an official report. I would like a detailed description of the jewellery, the Rolexes, and the paintings.'

'All right.'

'I would also like a complete list of those friends of yours who were informed of your movements, with their addresses and telephone numbers.'

The woman gave a little laugh.

'You don't suspect them, I hope?'

Montalbano looked at her.

'Do you think they'll be offended?'

'Absolutely.'

'Then don't tell them anything. I'll be the first. See you later, at the station.'

TWO

The moment he walked into the station he noticed that Catarella looked pained and distressed.

'What's going on?'

'Nuttin', Chief.'

'You know you're supposed to tell me everything! Out with it! What happened?'

Catarella blew up.

'Chief, iss not my fault if Isspector Augello ghess let go! Iss not my fault if Fazio goes to da market! 'Oo's I asposta ax? 'Oo's I got left? Jess youse, Chief! An' ya treated me real bad!'

He was crying, and to keep Montalbano from seeing, he was turned three-quarters away as he spoke.

'I'm sorry, Cat, but this morning I was upset about something personal. You had nothing to do with it. I'm really sorry.'

The inspector had barely sat down at his desk when Fazio came in.

'Chief, sorry I wasn't available this morning, but there was a big row at the market . . .'

'Apparently this is the morning for excuses. Never mind, just sit down and let me tell you about this burglary.'

When Montalbano had finished, Fazio nodded several times.

'Strange,' he said.

'Well, it was certainly a perfectly planned burglary. We've never seen anything so well planned in Vigàta.'

Fazio was now shaking his head.

'I wasn't referring to the perfect planning, but to the perfect resemblance.'

'What do you mean?'

'Chief, just three days ago, there was another burglary just like this one, an exact duplicate.'

'Why wasn't I informed of this?'

'Because you told us you didn't want to be bothered with things like burglaries. Inspector Augello took care of it.'

'Tell me more.'

'Do you know a lawyer named Lojacono?'

'Emilio? A fat man, about fifty, with a limp?'

'That's him.'

'And so?'

'Every Saturday morning his wife goes to Ravanusa to visit her mother.'

'A fine example of daughterly devotion. What do I care if she visits her mother? What's that got to do with anything?'

'A lot. Just hang on a minute. Do you know a lady named Dr Vaccaro?'

'The pharmacist?'

'That's right. Her husband also goes to see his mother every Saturday morning, in Favara.'

Montalbano was starting to feel his nerves fraying. 'Would you please get to the point?'

'I'm getting to that. So anyway, both Lojacono the lawyer and Dr Vaccaro the pharmacist take advantage of the absence of their respective spouses and every Saturday spend a blissful night in Lojacono's country house.'

'How long have they been lovers?'

'For a little over a year.'

'And who knows about it?'

'Everyone in town.'

'We're off to a good start. So how'd it go?'

'The lawyer's a man known for being precise; he always does the same things, never varies. For instance, when he goes to his country house with his lover, he always leaves the keys on top of the television, which is only about three feet away from a window that is always left half open, night and day, winter and summer. Got that?'

'Got it.'

'The burglars stuck a wooden pole about ten feet long with a magnetic metal tip through the railing and through the window, attracted the keys with the magnet, and then took them.'

'How did you find out about the pole?'

'We found it at the scene.'

'Go on.'

'Then they opened the gate and front door with the keys and, without making any noise, went into the bedroom and gassed the lawyer and the lady pharmacist. They grabbed all the valuables they could find, then got into both cars, since the lady had come in her own, and drove here to Vigàta to ransack their homes.'

'So there were at least three burglars.'

'Why do you say that?'

'Because there had to have been a third man, the one driving the burglars' own car.'

'True.'

'Can you explain to me why none of the local TV stations ever mentioned this story?'

'Because we did a great job. We wanted to avoid a scandal.'

At that moment Catarella showed up.

'Beckin' yer partin', Chief, but Misser an' Missis Piritone juss come onna premisses juss now.'

Montalbano gave Catarella a dirty look but decided not to say anything. He might start crying again.

'Is that really their name?' Fazio asked in disbelief.

'Of course not! Their name's Peritore. Listen, take them into your office, get their report and the list they've drawn up, and then come back here.'

*

After spending the next half-hour signing papers, which were piling up on his desk out of control, the telephone rang.

'Chief, 'at'd be yer lady frenn.'

'Is she here?'

'Nossir, she's onna line.'

'Tell her I'm not here.'

Catarella must have balked.

'Chief, beckin' yer partin' an' all, bu' mebbe ya din't unnastand 'oo's onna line. The foresaid caller in quession is yer lady frenn Livia, I dunno if 'at wuz clear t'yiz.'

'I got that, Cat. I'm not here.'

'Whate'er y' say, Chief.'

And immediately Montalbano regretted it. What kind of nonsense was this, anyway? He was acting like a little boy who'd quarrelled with a little girl in the playground. How was he going to fix it? He had an idea.

He got up and went to Catarella's station. 'Let me use your mobile phone for a second.'

Catarella handed it to him, and Montalbano headed to the car park, got into his car, started it up, and drove off. When he was in the middle of traffic, he called Livia.

'Hello, Livia? Salvo here. Catarella told me . . . I'm in the car, so make it quick.'

'Well, hats off to your Adelina!' Livia began.

'Why, what did she do?'

'First of all, she suddenly appeared before me when I was naked! She didn't even knock!'

'Wait a second, why should she have knocked? She didn't know you were there, and since she has a set of keys . . .'

'You always defend her! And do you know what she said the moment she saw me?'

'No.'

'She said – or at least this is what it sounded like she said, since she speaks that African dialect of yours (Livia loved to be rude about his native Sicilian tongue): "Oh, you're here? Then I'm leaving. Goodbye." And she turned on her heel and left!'

Montalbano decided to let the business of the 'African dialect' slide.

'Livia, you know perfectly well that Adelina has trouble with you. It's an old story. Is it possible that every time—'

'It certainly is possible! And I have trouble with her too!'

'Then can't you see she was right to leave?'

'Let's just drop it, OK? I'm going to take the bus into Vigàta.'

'What for?'

'To go shopping. Do you want lunch or not?'

'Of course I want lunch! But why do you want to go to all the trouble? You came here to have a couple of days off, no?'

What a stinking hypocrite. The truth of the matter was that Livia didn't know how to cook, and every time he ate something she'd made, he felt poisoned.

'So what should we do?'

'I'll come by with the car around one and we'll go to Enzo's. And in the meantime enjoy the sunshine.'

'I've got all the sun I need at home in Boccadasse.'

'I don't doubt that for a minute. But I've got a possible solution. Here you could take the sunlight from the front, on your face and tummy, let's say, and in Boccadasse you could take it from behind, on your back, that is.'

It had slipped out. He bit his tongue.

'What's this nonsense?' asked Livia.

'Nothing. Sorry, I was just trying to be funny. See you later.'

He went back to his office.

*

Fazio returned after about an hour.

'All taken care of. It took a while. I must say the burg-lars certainly did well on this one!'

'And the one before?'

'There were fewer valuables there, but totalling up the things they found in both houses, I'd say things went pretty well there, too.'

'They must have a coordinator who knows what he's doing.'

'The brains of the gang isn't too bad, either.'

'I'm sure we'll be hearing from them again. Did you get the list of their friends?'

'Yes.'

'This afternoon I want you to start checking them out, one by one.'

'All right. Oh, and I made a copy for you.' He laid a sheet of paper down on the desk.

'A copy of what?'

'The list of the Peritores' friends.'

*

After Fazio left, the inspector decided to ring Adelina.

'Why dinna you tella me 'atta you girlfrenn was acomin?' the housekeeper attacked him.

'Because I didn't know she was coming, either. It was a surprise.'

'Well, she mekka me a bigga sahprize too! Alla nekkid like a she was!'

'Listen, Adelì . . .'

'An' whenna she gonna go?'

'Probably in two or three days. Don't worry, I'll let you know. Listen, is your son free?'

'Which one?'

'Pasquale.'

Adelina's two sons, Giuseppe and Pasquale, were two incorrigible delinquents forever in and out of prison.

Pasquale, who Montalbano had even arrested a few times, was particularly fond of the inspector and had asked him, to Livia's great shock and dismay, to be his son's godfather and baptize him.

'Yeh, fadda moment 'e's free. Bu' no' Giuseppe. 'E's in jail in Palermo.'

'Could you ask Pasquale if he could come down to the station this afternoon, say around four?'

'Wha' fah? You wanna 'rrest 'im?' Adelina was alarmed.

'Don't worry, Adelì. You have my word of honour. I just want to talk to him.'

'OK, whativva you say.'

*

He went home to pick up Livia, who he found on the veranda, reading a book, surly and silent.

'Where do you want to go?'

'I dunno.'

'Shall we go to Enzo's?'

'I dunno.'

'How about Carlo's?'

There was no restaurant in the area by that name, but seeing the welcome Livia was giving him, he'd decided to go on the offensive.

And whatever happened, happened.

'I dunno,' Livia said for the third time, indifferent. She hadn't even blinked at the sound of that name.

'Well, I say we go to Enzo's and end the discussion.'

Livia kept reading her book for another five minutes, purely out of spite, leaving Montalbano standing beside her.

☆

As they entered the trattoria, Enzo, the owner, came running up to Livia to pay his respects.

'What a lovely surprise! It's so good to see you again!'

'Thank you.'

'You're a sight for sore eyes! A true delight! Can you explain to me how it is that every time you honour me by coming here, you're always more beautiful than the last?'

Like a ray of sunshine, a sudden smile swept the clouds away from Livia's face.

But how was it that the Sicilian dialect was suddenly

no longer African and now quite comprehensible? Montalbano wondered.

'What would you like?' Enzo asked.

'I do feel a little hungry,' said Livia.

And if Enzo's compliments ended up whetting her
appetite, just imagine the effect Carlo's compliments must
have!

Montalbano's irritation doubled.

'I've got spaghetti in a sauce of sea urchin, fresh as can
be, caught just this morning, a real treat,' said Enzo.

'Then let's go with the sea urchin,' Livia consented,
batting her eyelashes like Minnie Mouse to Mickey.

'And what do you feel like?' Enzo asked the inspector.

*I feel like taking this fork and gouging out both of my girlfriend's
eyes*, Montalbano thought to himself.

Instead he said: 'I'm not very hungry myself. Just bring
me some antipasti.'

After wolfing her spaghetti, Livia smiled at her boyfriend and put her hand on top of his, caressing it.

'I apologize for last night.'

'For last night?' said Montalbano, as phony as a
twelve-pound note, pretending not to remember anything.

'Yes, for last night. I really acted stupidly.'

Oh, no you don't! That shouldn't count! It wasn't fair!
Montalbano felt outmanoeuvred.

He made a gesture with his other hand that meant
nothing and everything, then muttered something.

Livia took it to mean they had made peace.

When they left the trattoria, Livia said she wanted to go to Montelusa, where she hadn't set foot for a long time.

'Go ahead and take the car,' said Montalbano.

'What about you?'

'I don't need it.'

*

He had no need to take his customary digestive and meditative stroll along the jetty to the lighthouse because he'd hardly eaten anything.

The fact that Livia had put him in a situation in which he couldn't bring up Carlo had closed off his stomach.

But he went for the stroll anyway, in the hopes of working off his irritation.

When he sat down on the flat rock under the lighthouse, however, his eye fell on the great tower dominating the landscape.

It had been built by Carlo V.

How many Carlos were there in the world, anyway?

*

Seeing him walk in, Catarella started gesticulating wildly.

'Ahh, Chief! There'd be 'at son o' yer cleanin' lady waitin' f' yiz! Says ya summonsed 'im!'

'Send him to me.'

The inspector went into his office, sat down at his desk, and Pasquale appeared.

'How's the little boy?'

''E's beautiful and growing.'

'And your wife?'

'Good. An' Miss Livia?'

'Fine, thanks.'

The ritual over, Pasquale got down to business.

'My mama tol' me—'

'Right, I need to ask you something. Have a seat.'

Pasquale sat.

'What is it?'

'Have you by any chance heard anything about these recent burglaries that were pulled off with such skill?'

Pasquale put on a distracted air, then twisted up his mouth, as if to minimize what he was about to say.

'Yessir. I've heard a couple o' li'l things.'

'What kinds of "little things"?'

'Well, you know, the kinds of things people say . . . an' you just happen to hear . . . in passing . . .'

'And what did you just happen to hear in passing?'

'Inspector, if I tell you, iss gotta remain between us, OK?'

'Of course.'

'I heard that it wasn't none of our people.'

That is, it didn't involve any thieves from Vigàta. 'I'd worked that out myself.'

'These people are real artists.'

'Right. Foreigners?'

'No, sir.'

'Northerners?'

'No, sir.'

'Who, then?'

'Sicilians, just like me an' you.'

'From the province?'

'Yessir.'

He was going to have to force it out of him. Pasquale obviously didn't like discussing the subject.

Being friends was one thing, playing informer was another.

Anyway, with cops, the less said the better.

'And why, in your opinion, did they suddenly decide to come and work in Vigàta?'

Before answering, Pasquale stared at his toecaps, then looked up at the ceiling, then finally decided to open his mouth.

'They were called.'

Called? Pasquale had said it so softly that Montalbano didn't understand.

'Speak louder.'

'They were called.'

'Explain what you mean.'

Pasquale threw his hands up.

'Inspector, all I heard is they were called directly by

someone from here, from Vigàta. An' he's their coordinator.'

'So this gentleman is both their mastermind and manager?'

'It looks that way.'

It wasn't that unusual for a gang of thieves to go somewhere on assignment, but he'd never heard of a crew being specifically enlisted for a job.

'Is he a thief himself?'

'I don' think so.'

Alas. If he wasn't a professional thief, that complicated matters considerably.

Who could he be?

And why did he do it?

THREE

'So, what do you make of it, Pasquà?'

'In what sense, Inspector?'

'Let's say, from your perspective.' As a thief, that is.

Pasquale smiled.

'You seen that pole, Inspector?'

'What pole?'

'The one with a magnet at the end, the one they used in the first burglary.'

'No, I haven't seen it. Have you?'

Pasquale's smile became even more amused.

'C'mon, Inspector, you still settin' up these li'l traps for me? If I seen the pole, it means I'm one of the gang.'

'Sorry, Pasquà, it just escaped me.'

'Well, I din't see it either, but somebody tol' me about it.'

'What's it like?'

'Iss made out of some special kind of wood, light and

strong, like bamboo, but it telescopes. You know what I mean? Iss a tool made just for that purpose, so I think you'd wanna keep it to use again.'

'And so?'

'Can you explain to me why they left it there, after the burglary? I woulda taken it with me. If iss like a telescope, iss not even hard to carry.'

'Did you know they even left behind the keys used in this morning's burglary?'

'No, I din't know. An' that don' make no sense to me, neither. A set o' keys is always useful.'

'Listen, Pasquà, one last question. The burglars also stole three cars. Did you know?'

'Yeah.'

'What did they do with them?'

'In my opinion, Inspector, they got rid of them and even made some money on them.'

'How?'

'If they're luxury cars, there's people that buy them to take them abroad.'

'And if they're not?'

'There's always car breakers who pay good money for spare parts.'

'Do you know any?'

'Any what?'

'Car breakers.'

'That's not my line.'

'OK. Have you anything else to tell me?'

'Nah.'

'All right, you can go. Thanks, Pasquà.'

'My respects, Inspector.'

✵

The inspector had realized immediately that the burglaries were the work of outsiders, skilled professionals. Vigàta's burglars were less sophisticated; they just broke down the door and went inside, but never when there were people at home, and never in a million years would they have thought to make a pole like the one used in the first burglary.

The gang must have consisted of four people: three outsiders working in the field and a fourth who was the brains of the outfit. And who was perhaps the only one living in Vigàta. Once the job was done, the others quite probably went back where they came from.

Montalbano's nose and experience told him this was going to be a difficult case.

His eye fell on the sheet of paper Fazio had left with him, with the list of the Peritores' friends' names. There were eighteen in all.

He started skimming it distractedly until the fourth name made him jump out of his chair.

Emilio Lojacono, lawyer.

The man who was at his country house with his lover

when his place in town was burgled first. Montalbano kept reading, paying closer attention.

At the seventeenth name, he gave another start. Dr Ersilia Vaccaro.

Lojacono's lover.

A lightning bolt shot across his brain.

An illogical intuition that the next burglary would surely involve one of the remaining sixteen names on the list.

And therefore what Fazio reported to him on the Peritores' friends would prove extremely important.

At that exact moment, Fazio rang. 'Chief, I wanted to tell you—'

'Just listen to me first. On that list of the Peritores' friends, did you notice—'

' – the names of Lojacono the lawyer and Dr Vaccaro? Absolutely! It was the first thing I saw!'

'And what do you think?'

'That the name of the next person to be burgled is on that list.'

Oh, well. He'd wanted to look brilliant, but it hadn't worked. It was one of those days where he was destined to be wrong-footed by everybody. On the other hand, Fazio often arrived at the same conclusions as him.

'What did you want to tell me?'

'Well, I found out that Livia is here with you.'

'Yes.'

'My wife would love it if you came to dinner at our place tomorrow night. If that's all right with you.'

Why wouldn't it be all right with him?

On top of everything else, Mrs Fazio was an excellent cook, a hardly negligible fact.

'Thanks, I'll tell Livia. We'd love to come. See you in the morning.'

*

'Catarella!'

'Yessir, Chief!'

'Come to my office, on the double.'

He hadn't even put the receiver down before Catarella materialized before him, bolt upright, at attention.

'Cat, I need to ask you to do something that shouldn't take you more than five minutes at the computer.'

'Chief, I'd sit in fronna a ka-pewter f'r a hunnert years f' yiz, sir!'

'I want you to make me a list of all the car breakers in our province who've been charged with receiving.'

Catarella looked flummoxed. 'I don' unnastan', Chief.'

'All of it or part of it?'

'Part of it.'

'Which one?'

'The ting about risseevin'.'

'Receiving?'

'Yeah. Wha'ss it mean?'

'It means buying or receiving stolen goods.'

'OK, Chief, bu' if iss bad, why's it goods?'

'Never mind,' said Montalbano, handing him a piece of paper with the word Receivers written at the top. 'Listen, get Fazio for me, would you?'

＊

The telephone rang. 'What is it, Chief?'

'Do you remember the models and licence plates of the three stolen cars?'

'No. But if you go into my office, there's a sheet of paper on the desk with everything written down on it.'

Fazio was very orderly, almost to a fault, and Montalbano found the page without effort.

He copied down the information and returned to his office.

> *Daewoo – CZ 566 RT – Dr Vaccaro*
>
> *Volvo – AC 641 RT – Lojacono the lawyer*
>
> *Fiat Panda – AV 872 RT – Mr Peritore*

When it came to cars, Montalbano understood about as much as he did about astrophysics, but he was certain that none of these was a luxury model.

Not five minutes later, Catarella came in and put a sheet of paper on his desk.

1) *Gemellaro, Angelo,*
   Via Garibaldi 32, Montereale, tel. 0922 4343217.
   Garage: Via Martiri di Belfiore 82. One conviction.

2) *Butticè, Carlo,*
   Via Etna 38, Sicudiana, tel. 0922 469521.
   Garage: Via Gioberti 79. One conviction.

3) *Macaluso, Carlo,*
   Viale Milizie 92, Montelusa, tel. 0922 2376594.
   Garage: Via Saracino (no number). Two convictions.

There you go: out of three crooks, two were named Carlo. This surely must mean something. Statistics never lied.

Of course, sometimes statisticians came up with findings fit for the loony bin, but in general . . .

There wasn't a minute to lose. The burglars probably hadn't placed the Peritores' car anywhere yet.

'Catarella, get me Prosecutor Tommaseo on the line.'

He had enough time to review the seven times table.

'What can I do for you, Montalbano?'

'Could I come and talk to you in about twenty minutes?'

'Sure, come right over.'

He put the list of the three breakers in his jacket pocket, called Gallo, and headed for Montelusa in a squad car.

It took him a good hour to persuade Tommaseo to put a tap on the three telephones.

Normally whenever anyone brought up phone tapping, the prosecutor curled up like a hedgehog. What if it turned out that a thief, drug dealer, or pimp was a close friend of a member of parliament? There would be hell to pay for the poor prosecutor.

The government was therefore trying to push through a law that would make all wiretapping illegal, but luckily they hadn't succeeded yet.

Montalbano returned to headquarters satisfied.

*

Less than five minutes after he'd sat down at his desk, the telephone rang.

'Ah, Chief, 'at be yer lady frenn 'at tol' me as how she's waitin' f' yiz inna car park, but I quickly sez straightaways 'at you wasn't here an' so she — she meanin' yer lady frenn — sez to me as how she's gonna wait f' yiz anyways. So wha' do we do now?'

'But why'd you tell her I wasn't here?'

''Cuz this mornin' 'arse whatcha tol' me ta say.'

'But it's not this morning any more!'

''Ass true, Chief. But ya nivver cunnermannit the order. 'N' so I din't know if yer diff'rinces wit' the lady was a timprary or poimanent state o' fairs.'

'Listen, go and see where she's parked.'

Catarella returned immediately to the phone. 'She's right ousside th'intrince gate.'

The only hope was to attempt an escape as if under siege. 'Is the back door of the building unlocked?'

'Nossir, iss always lacked.'

'What a pain! And who has the key?'

'I do, Chief.'

'Go and open it.'

Montalbano got up, travelled all the way across the building, and came to the door, which Catarella was holding open for him.

He went out onto the street, turned the corner, turned another corner, and came out in front of the gate.

Upon seeing him, Livia gave a light toot of the horn. Montalbano smiled and got into the car.

'Been waiting long?'

'Barely five minutes.'

'Where are we going?'

'Do you mind if we go home first? I want to have a shower.'

✶

While Livia was in the bathroom, Montalbano sat out on the veranda, enjoying the evening and smoking a cigarette.

Livia then appeared, ready to go out.

'Where do you want to go?' Montalbano asked.

'You decide.'

'I'd like to go to a place where I've never been before. It's by the sea, past Montereale. Enzo told me the food's really good.'

'Well, if Enzo says so . . .'

Someone who knew the way would have made it there in about twenty minutes. Montalbano, who took four wrong turns, took exactly an hour.

To top things off, he had a heated argument with Livia, who had actually suggested the right way to go.

It was a proper restaurant with waiters in uniform and pictures of football players and pop singers on the walls.

To get away from it all, they chose a table on the terrace over the sea.

The place was packed with British tourists already half drunk on sea air.

Salvo and Livia had to wait a good fifteen minutes before a waiter arrived at their table, wearing a green nameplate on his lapel with Carlo spelled out in black letters.

The hair on the inspector's arms stood up as straight as the fur on an angry cat.

He made a lightning decision.

'Could you come back in five minutes?' he asked the waiter.

'Of course, sir, as you wish.'

Livia gave him a puzzled look. 'What's wrong?'

'I have to run to the loo.'

He stood up and dashed off before Livia's stunned eyes.

'Where's the manager?' he asked a waiter.

'At the cash register.'

He went to the cash register. There was a man of about sixty with an Umbertine moustache and gold-rimmed glasses.

'What can I do for you, sir?'

'I'm Inspector Montalbano.'

'What a pleasure! My good friend Enzo—'

'I'm terribly sorry, but I'm in something of a hurry. The lady who's with me lost her beloved brother ten days ago, whose name was Carlo. The waiter assigned to our table is also called Carlo, and I wouldn't want . . . you understand . . .'

'I certainly do understand, Inspector, I'll send another waiter right away.'

'I thank you from the bottom of my heart.' He went and sat back down, smiling at Livia. 'Sorry. A sudden, urgent need.'

A new waiter arrived. His name tag said Giorgio. They ordered their antipasti.

'Wasn't the first waiter named Carlo?' Livia asked.

'Was he? I hadn't noticed.'

'I wonder why they changed.'

'Do you mind?'

'Why should I mind?'

'I dunno, you seem to regret it.'

'What are you saying! He was just a little cuter.'

'Cuter! Then maybe it's better this way, no?'

Livia looked at him, feeling more and more puzzled. 'You mean better that they changed waiters?'

'Exactly.'

'Why?'

'Because over sixty per cent of the people named Carlo are criminals. It's a statistical fact.'

He realized he was talking complete rubbish, but his rage and jealousy prevented him from reasoning in any way. He couldn't help himself.

'Oh, come on!'

'So don't believe it, if you don't want to. Do you know many men called Carlo?'

'A few.'

'And are they all criminals?'

'What has got into you, Salvo?'

'Into me? Into you, rather! You're making such a big deal out of this Carlo! If you like, we can have your Carlo come back!'

'Have you lost your mind?'

'No, I haven't lost my mind! It's you who—'

'And here are the antipasti,' said the waiter, suddenly appearing.

Livia waited for him to leave before speaking.

'Listen to me, Salvo. Yesterday I was the one acting

like an idiot, but tonight you seem to be trying your hardest to outdo me. Now I'm telling you that I have no desire to spend my evenings here arguing with you. If you keep carrying on this way, I'm going to call a cab, go back to Marinella, pack my suitcase, and continue on to Palermo and catch the first plane heading north. You decide.'

Montalbano, who already felt ashamed for the previous scene, said only:

'Just try the antipasti. They look really good.'

The first course was also good.

And the second too.

And two bottles of excellent wine did their part. They came out of the restaurant holding hands.

That night, their reconciliation was long and perfect.

*

At eight o'clock the next morning, he was ready to go out when the phone rang.

It was Catarella.

'Somebody get killed?'

'Nobody's killed, Chief, sorry 'bout that. But the c'mishner's affice called askin' yiz to drap in sayin' iss pretty oijent.'

'Who was it that called?'

''Ey din't say, Chief. 'Ey jess say you's asposta go tadda place where they keep the wine.'

'What's that supposed to be, a winery?'

'Well, 'arse what they tol' me, Chief.'

'Did they really say "the place where they keep the wine", or did they use another word?'

'A nutter woid, Chief.'

'The cellar?'

''Ass it!'

The cellar was what they called the basement area where they kept all the phone-tapping equipment.

'If Fazio comes in, tell him to wait for me.'

'Yessir, Chief.'

He said goodbye to Livia and headed off for Montelusa.

*

The door to the basement was armour-plated and had a guard armed with a machine gun posted outside.

'Are your orders to shoot all journalists on sight?'

'Who are you?' asked the guard, who was in no mood for jokes.

'Inspector Montalbano.'

'Papers, please.'

Montalbano showed him his ID, and the young man opened the door and said:

'Box seven.'

He knocked on the door of box seven, which was only

slightly larger than a voting booth, and a voice inside told him to come in.

Inside was a chief inspector sitting in front of a machine with a set of headphones around his neck.

He stood up and introduced himself. 'Guarnera.'

'Montalbano.'

'This morning at six-thirteen there was an interesting phone call to a subscriber named Carlo Macaluso. You should listen to it. Here, put on this headset.' He turned a knob, and Montalbano heard a sleepy voice, which must have been Macaluso's, saying:

'Hello? Who is this?'

'I'm the friend with the moustache,' a young-sounding voice replied decisively.

'Oh, is something up?'

'I got three brand-new packages.'

'I'm interested. What do we do?'

'The usual. Tonight at midnight we'll leave them in the usual place.'

'All right, and I'll leave the money there. The usual amount.'

'No. This stuff's brand new.'

'Tell you what. I'll give you the usual amount, and then make up the difference next time. OK?'

'OK.'

FOUR

Montalbano took the headset off, thanked Guarnera, said goodbye, and headed back to the station.

He'd been lucky. If nothing else, the cars would be returned to their rightful owners.

He went straight to Fazio's office. 'Come with me.'

Fazio got up and followed him. 'Take a seat.'

He told him what Pasquale had said, how he'd got the idea of looking into the car breakers, and the phone conversation he'd just heard.

'How should we proceed?' Fazio asked.

'Obviously, starting this afternoon, we need to begin following Macaluso.'

'I'll send Gallo, who can stay in touch with us via mobile phone.'

'Sounds good.'

'Maybe we ought to postpone tonight's dinner.'

'Why? If we start eating at eight-thirty, Gallo is sure

not to call before ten-thirty, eleven. If anything comes up, Livia can stay with your wife, and when we've finished, I'll come and pick her up, even if it's a bit late.'

'OK.'

'But you should send three other men with Gallo.'

'Why?'

'Because Macaluso will surely have three men with him, to drive the other cars.'

'You're right.'

'Now tell me if you've found out anything interesting about the Peritores' friends.'

'Chief, so far I've made it halfway down the list, and, aside from the names of Lojacono and Dr Vaccaro, which you already noticed, I found number five rather interesting. Have a look at the list.'

It was on the desk. Montalbano slid it over and looked at it. Number five was Giancarlo de Martino, engineer. 'So who is he?'

'An outsider, born in Mantua.'

'And what's he doing here?'

'He's been living in Vigàta for four years. He's in charge of the harbour reconstruction.'

'So why do you say he's interesting?'

'Because he spent four years in jail.'

Four years was no joke.

'What'd he do?'

'Aiding and abetting an armed gang.'

'Like the Red Brigades or something similar?'

'That's right.'

'And how did he aid and abet them?'

Fazio smiled.

'He organized burglaries to finance them.'

'Shit!'

'Precisely.'

'But how old is he?'

'Exactly sixty years old.'

'What do people around town say about him?'

'That he's a respectable, mild-mannered man.'

'As far as that goes, I'm sure when we arrest the brains of the gang we'll find out that he, too, is a respectable, mild-mannered man.'

'Sure, Chief, but de Martino has become a man of order. He votes for the governing party and does advertising for the PdL.'

'Then we should keep a doubly close watch over him.'

'Already taken care of, Chief. I've got Officer Caruana looking after him.'

'All right then, but carry on with that list; it's important. See you this evening, at your place.'

*

He went off to Marinella to pick up Livia, but didn't find her at home. Looking out from the veranda, he saw her lying on the beach in her swimsuit near the water's edge. He walked down to greet her.

'I'm sunbathing.'

'I can see that. But get dressed now; we're going out to eat.'

'I don't feel like getting dressed.'

'Well, I happen to be a little hungry.'

'I've seen to everything.'

Montalbano turned pale. He was worn out.

If Livia had cooked, he would have a stomach ache for two days, guaranteed.

'I called the *rosticceria*; they were very nice. What do you call that pizza you make around here?'

Calling *cuddriruni* pizza was sheer blasphemy. Like calling *arancini*, *suppli*.

'*Cuddriruni.*'

'I explained it to them, and they worked it out. And there's roast chicken and French fries too. They delivered it. It's all in the oven.'

'I'll take care of it,' the inspector said impulsively, energized by the narrow escape. 'You go ahead and continue sunbathing.'

He went into the house, put on his trunks, laid the table on the veranda, and dived into the sea. The water was cold but invigorating. He went back inside, dried himself, and called Livia.

After eating, they went back down to the beach and lay down.

*

Since he'd dozed off and Livia hadn't woken him up, he returned to the office a little late, around four-thirty.

'Any news?' he asked Catarella.

'Nuttin', Chief.'

'Get Fazio on the line and put him through to me.'

He sat down behind his desk, which was covered by a mountain of papers to be signed.

To sign or not to sign? That was the question. And what about Fazio? Why no news of him? He called Catarella.

'Ah, Chief! Fazio musta toined hisself off insomuch as the attamatic young lady tol' me attamatically 'at the poisson I's tryin' a reach's available.'

'You mean "unavailable".'

'Why, wha'd I say?'

'Listen, as soon as he answers, put him through to me.'

After thinking it over, he decided to listen to his bureaucratic conscience and start signing his name a hundred or so times.

About an hour later, the phone rang. It was Fazio. 'Sorry, Chief, I was involved in a delicate discussion with someone to do with the list. I'll tell you later.'

'What's the situation?'

'All in order. Gallo's got Macaluso's garage under surveillance, and at seven this evening he'll be joined by Miccichè, Tantillo, and Vadalà.'

'So, see you at eight-thirty, then.'

*

He resumed signing papers, but after about fifteen minutes, he was interrupted by the phone again.

'Ah, Chief, there'd be a jinnelman onna premises 'at wants a talk t'yiz poissonally in poisson.'

'What does he want?'

''E sez 'is home was buggerized.'

Another burglary? Burglaries, at that moment, took absolute priority over everything else.

'Send him to me at once.'

There was a gentle knock at the door.

'Come in!'

'Hello, my name is Giosuè Incardona,' the man said as he walked in.

Montalbano shot a quick glance at the list of the Peritores' friends: no Incardona.

'Please sit down.'

The man looked about fifty, wore very thick glasses, hadn't a single hair on his head, was quite thin, and wore clothes too big for him. Being in a police station clearly made him nervous.

'I don't mean to disturb, but . . .'

'What can I do for you?'

'I have a small house in the country halfway to Montelusa. Now and then I go there with my wife and two grandchildren. Last time I went I left my reading glasses there, and so this afternoon I went back and found the front door broken in.'

'What do you mean by "broken in"?'

'It was off its hinges.'

'Would it have been so difficult to pick the lock or use a skeleton key?'

'No, sir, easy as pie. Apparently they didn't want to waste any time.'

'What did they steal?'

'The brand-new television set, a computer we use to play films for our grandchildren, an eighteenth-century watch that used to belong to my great-grandfather, and that's all. But they were looking for something else, if you ask me.'

'What were they looking for?'

'These.'

He extracted a set of keys from his pocket and showed them to the inspector.

'What are they for?'

'They're for my home here in Vigàta. The robbers must've known that I keep a set in the country. And I'm sure that if they'd found them, they'd've come and burgled our house here.'

'And why didn't they find them?'

'Because the last time I was there, I put them in a different place. I put them in the cistern. I'd just finished watching *The Godfather*. Remember the scene where the Godfather's son goes to kill the . . .'

Montalbano picked up the list of names and handed it to Incardona.

'Have a look at this list, if you don't mind, and tell me if you know any of these individuals.'

Incardona took it, looked at it, and handed it back to Montalbano.

'Almost all of them.'

Montalbano gave a start. 'How is that?'

'In all modesty, I'm the best plumber in town. And I also make perfect copies of keys.'

'Listen, do you remember whether you advised any of these people to do as you do – that is, to keep an extra set of keys available at a different residence?'

'Of course! It's the surest way to—'

'Excuse me for just a minute.'

He called Catarella.

'Please accompany this gentleman to Galluzzo's desk and have Galluzzo draw up his statement. Mr Incardona, if there are any new developments, you'll be the first to know. Thank you so much.'

There was something about this that didn't make sense.

This latest burglary was almost certainly a red herring intended to throw him off the scent.

In speaking to their friends, the Peritores must have mentioned that they'd given the police their names.

And the brains of the outfit, hoping to prevent Montalbano from reaching a certain conclusion, had created a diversion. Except that it had come too late.

And the three agents in the field had made the mistake of breaking in the door. Apparently they knew it was a job that wouldn't net much, carried out just to throw up a smokescreen.

Another mistake was made by the brains himself, by choosing, as the victim of the bogus burglary or whatever it was, someone who wasn't on the list but was known by everyone on it.

This meant that the next real burglary would occur at the home of one of the sixteen people whose names were on the list.

The mastermind of the ring was showing that he had a brain that ran at very high speed and understood the way the inspector's brain worked.

It was going to be a thrilling game of chess.

✡

When he went to pick up Livia, he noticed she was wearing an outfit he hadn't seen before. A pleated skirt and elegant blouse, Thirties-style, with two sorts of flounces in front.

'Nice outfit,' he said.

'Do you like it? A friend of mine made it for me; he's a tailor. He wanted to put some flounces hanging from behind, too, but to me it seemed a little excessive.'

It was not a flash, but a veritable lightning bolt, zigzagging through space, followed by a deafening thunderclap, that struck and nearly burned up the inspector's brain, leaving him dazed and numb.

Livia was worried. 'What's wrong?'

'Nothing, just a slight dizzy feeling. I must be tired. Tell me something: is your tailor's name Carlo?'

'Yes, and for your information, he's not a criminal,' Livia replied defensively. 'Actually he's a wonderful, honest person,' she continued. 'But how did you guess his name?'

'Guess? I didn't guess anything. You told me yourself.'

'Really? I don't remember. Shall we go?

*

THE REWARDS OF TRUST
A novel for girls from good families with strict customs.

A man consumed by jealousy distorts the meaning of something his woman says in her sleep and torments himself for days, subjecting her to interrogations, quarrels, and traps. Only when his insane jealousy subsides does he reap his rewards. In fact, the woman by chance reveals the true and entirely innocent meaning of the words she said in her sleep. And as of that moment, the man's love for the woman of his life increases manifold.

Not bad, eh? And instructive too.

✻

Mrs Fazio made simple but tasteful dishes. A fish soup and crispy fried mullet. And the cannoli Montalbano had brought were delicious.

In the presence of the two women, the inspector and Fazio did not talk about work.

At a quarter to eleven, Montalbano drove Livia back to Marinella with Fazio following behind, and then got into Fazio's car.

At ten past eleven, Fazio's mobile phone rang. It was Gallo. 'Macaluso's just left his house and taken the Vigàta road. He's driving a yellow Mitsubishi. There are three other men with him. I'm following behind. Where are you?'

'In Marinella.'

'If you ask me, he's headed for Montereale. If you stay where you are, we'll drive right past you. If he changes direction, I'll let you know.'

They positioned themselves at the end of Montalbano's access road, with headlights off and the nose of the car just off the main road.

About ten minutes later they saw a yellow Mitsubishi drive by.

Then, two cars behind the Mitsubishi, a Volkswagen Polo.

'That's Gallo's car,' said Fazio.

And he pulled out behind him.

'We're right behind you,' Fazio told him over the mobile phone.

'I saw you.'

They passed Montereale, then Sicudiana, then Montallegro. At ten minutes to twelve, Macaluso's car was still forging on.

Then they saw the Mitsubishi indicate right and go into a large sort of parking area.

As they drove past, Montalbano and Fazio noticed three other cars parked there.

'The other cars are already there,' said the inspector. At that moment Gallo shouted through the mobile phone: 'I'm going back! I'm gonna get them!'

A second later they saw his car coming towards them at an insane speed.

Fazio let him pass, then made a U-turn so fast that the car nearly turned over.

By the time they pulled into the parking area, Gallo already had the situation under control.

The three men had each managed to get into a car, but hadn't had the time to turn the key. They all stood with their hands in the air, as Gallo and the policemen with him had their guns trained on them.

Macaluso, standing near a municipal bin, also had his hands raised. In one hand he had a packet wrapped in newspaper and bound with a piece of string.

'I'll take that,' Montalbano said.

Macaluso gave it to him.

'How much is there?'

'Fifteen thousand euros in hundred-euro notes.'

To return to Vigàta, Montalbano had to drive Fazio's car.

*

'Since you were caught like a fool with three stolen cars — in other words, red-handed — I get the feeling, my dear Macaluso, that this time you're fucked,' said Fazio. ''Cause you're also a repeat offender, with two previous convictions for receiving stolen goods.'

The three accomplices had been taken to holding cells.

Macaluso, for his part, was on the grill in Montalbano's office.

'Could you take my handcuffs off?' asked Macaluso. He was a great big man in overalls, a sort of walking wardrobe, red-haired and red-skinned.

'No,' said Montalbano.

Silence fell.

'I can wait all night, if it comes to that,' said Fazio.

Macaluso sighed and began to speak.

'Things ain't what they look like,' he said.

'Chief, did you know our friend here was a philoso-pher?' said Fazio. 'Then tell us what things are really like.'

'I got a call from a customer that tol' me to go an' pick up these three cars he left—'

'The customer's name?' asked Fazio.

'I don' remember.'

'And how'd you get the keys?'

'He said he left 'em in the boot of the Daewoo, which was unlocked.'

'This detail may even be true, but I'm sure it was the thieves who left them there.'

'I assure you that—'

'Try to think up a better one, come on.'

'You know what I say?' Montalbano cut in. 'It's getting late. It's two o'clock in the morning. And I'm sleepy.'

'Lemme go an' we'll all go to bed,' Macaluso suggested.

'Quiet. Keep your mouth shut and listen to me,' said the inspector. 'Listen closely.'

And he started to recite from memory the intercepted phone conversation.

'*Hello? Who is this?*'

'*I'm the friend with the moustache.*'

'*Oh, is something up?*'

'*I got three brand-new packages . . .*' He looked at Macaluso and asked: 'Is that enough, or should I go on?'

'Th'arse enough.'

'Want a cigarette?'

'Yeah.'

Montalbano handed it to Fazio, who stuck it between Macaluso's lips and lit it for him.

'We can make a deal.'

'Le'ss hear it.'

'You tell us the name of the man on the phone, the one with the moustache, and I'll tell the prosecutor to take your cooperation into consideration.'

'I wish I could make that deal, believe me.'

'Who's preventing you?'

'Nobody. But this man wit' the moustache, I only seen 'im once, at night, real quick-like, three years ago, an' I don' even know 'is name.'

'How long have you been working with him?'

'Three years, like I said. They call, they tell me where they left the car, I put the money in the glove compartment, I leave, an' th'arse it.'

He seemed sincere.

FIVE

Montalbano exchanged a quick glance with Fazio and they both understood. Fazio was also of the opinion that Maca-luso was telling the truth.

Carrying on would only mean losing sleep.

'Put him in a holding cell,' the inspector said to Fazio. 'And tomorrow have them all taken to the prison, and send the report to Tommaseo. Good night.'

Montalbano wasn't happy with the way things had gone.

✳

'Wake up, lazybones!'

He slowly raised his eyelids, which seemed stuck together with glue. Through the open window a glorious sun beamed triumphant.

'Could you bring me a cup of coffee in bed?'

'No. But it's all ready in the kitchen.'

To take one's coffee lying down, God forbid!

A mortal sin worse than lust!

He got up, cursing to himself, went into the kitchen, drank his coffee, and then locked himself in the bathroom.

When he came back out, it was ten o'clock.

At the station, Fazio was waiting for him. 'Chief, I've got a few things to tell you.'

'Me too. You go first.'

'Yesterday, when you were trying to reach me on the mobile phone and found it turned off, I was in the middle of a discussion with Mrs Agata Cannavò, the widow of Commander Gesmundo Cannavò, ex-director general of the port, ex-sponsor of Dockers' Day, ex—'

'Fine, fine, but who's Mrs Cannavò?'

'The sixteenth name on the list.'

'Ah, right. And why did you go and talk to her?'

'I went to tell her that there was a possibility, however slim, that she would be burgled.'

'I don't understand.'

'Well, till now I'd been hearing about the people on the list from outsiders, and I was interested in finding out what somebody who was on the list thought about the whole thing.'

'Good idea! What did she say?'

'A whole slew of things. The widow is a busybody who knows everything about everyone. And she talks non-stop. She told me that Tavella, the accountant, is drowning in debt because he spends all his time in illegal gambling dens.

She told me that Mrs Martorana, the wife of Antonio Martorana, the surveyor, is the lover of de Martino, the engineer. And she told me in a whisper that the Peritores, in her opinion, have an "open" marriage, even though they do everything to hide it. To the point of going to church every Sunday. And she even told me something funny.'

'What was that?'

'Apparently, on the night the seaside house was burgled, there were four people sleeping there.'

'So? What's wrong with that?'

'Well, according to the widow, Mrs Peritore was in one bedroom with another man, while Mr Peritore was in a different bedroom with another woman.'

'But hadn't they gone there to celebrate their wedding anniversary?'

'I guess everyone has their own way of celebrating,' Fazio said philosophically.

'Nice little social circle. Listen, what's Peritore do for a living?'

'Officially speaking, he sells used cars.'

'And unofficially?'

'He lives off his wife, who's filthy rich from an inheritance an aunt left to her.'

'So, to conclude, the widow didn't tell you anything pertinent to the burglaries.'

'Nothing.'

'So we're at a dead end.'

''Fraid so.'

'I'm absolutely positive there's going to be another burglary.'

'Me too. But we can't very well put eleven apartments under surveillance here and another handful of villas and houses in the country or by the sea!'

'We'll just have to wait. And hope that they make some kind of mistake next time.'

'That's unlikely.'

'Not really. In the burglary that was supposed to throw us off, they made the mistake of breaking down the door.'

'What burglary was that, may I ask?'

'Ah, that's right, you were never informed.'

And he told Fazio about the visit of Incardona the plumber and the burglary that, according to him, was just a red herring.

Fazio agreed.

＊

When Fazio left, the inspector reached out with one hand, picked up the four letters addressed to him that he'd found on his desk, and started slowly studying the postmarks.

Two had been sent from Milan, another from Rome, and the last one from Montelusa.

In Milan he had no friends; in Rome he had a friend who had even put him up once, but he'd been recently transferred to Parma; and in Montelusa, of course, he knew a lot of people.

But the truth of the matter was that he hated to open his post.

Nowadays he received all sorts of advertising pamphlets, invitations to cultural events, and occasionally a few meagre lines from former schoolmates of his.

All things considered, given his age, he had to admit he hadn't made many friends over the course of his life.

In a way he was happy about this, and in another way he wasn't. Perhaps, with old age coming on faster than a rocket heading for outer space, it would have been better to have a few friends by his side.

But, deep down, weren't Fazio, Mimì Augello, and even Catarella by now more friends than colleagues?

This was his consolation, if there was indeed any consolation in it.

He decided to open the letters.

Three of them were of no importance, but the fourth . . .

It was anonymous, and written in block capitals.

It went as follows:

MY DEAR INSPECTOR,

PLEASE CONSIDER THIS LETTER A SORT OF GAUNTLET THAT I AM THROWING DOWN.

AT ANY RATE YOU HAVE ALREADY ACCEPTED

THE CHALLENGE BY TAKING ON THE INVESTIGATION
PERSONALLY.

AND SO I HAVE THE PLEASURE OF INFORMING YOU
THAT, UNFORTUNATELY FOR YOU, THERE WILL BE TWO MORE
BURGLARIES.

AFTER WHICH I SHALL GO BACK TO DOING WHAT I HAVE
ALWAYS DONE.

BUT I WILL HAVE HAD A LOT OF FUN. I'M ENTITLED TO
HAVE A PASTIME LIKE ANYONE ELSE, AM I NOT?

AND THE FACT THAT I'M DOING THIS JUST TO AMUSE
MYSELF IS CLEAR FROM THE FACT THAT I LET MY
COLLABORATORS KEEP ALL THE LOOT.

IT IS UP TO YOU TO PREVENT THE NEXT TWO
BURGLARIES, WHICH YOU CAN DO ONLY BY GUESSING THE
TIME AND PLACE.

CORDIALLY YOURS, AND WITH BEST WISHES.

The letter had been sent from Montelusa the day before.

The inspector called Fazio and handed it to him. Fazio read it and put it back on the desk without saying anything.

'What do you think?'

Fazio shook his head.

'Bah!'

'Come on, don't talk like the Sibyl. Speak!'

'Chief, this letter seems totally useless to me. The man wrote it just to write it. It has no purpose.'

'So it would seem, to all appearances.'

'Whereas?'

'Well, first of all, it's clear that the man who sent it is pretentious. He may even be quite intelligent, but he's definitely pretentious. And pretentious people can't always control themselves. At some point they can't help but try and show, whatever the cost, that they're better than everyone else.'

'And second?'

'Second, he wants us to think that these burglaries are only an amusement, a pastime of his.'

'Whereas?'

'Whereas I'm under the impression that he's looking for something, something specific, just one thing, the only thing he's interested in.'

'Something to steal?'

'Not necessarily. Sometimes these burglaries have, well, collateral damage. When I was a deputy inspector, a house was robbed. The lady came and declared all the jewellery she lost. And then by chance, her husband saw the list. And he realized that there were a couple of earrings and a necklace that he hadn't given her. It was her lover that had bought them for her. And the whole thing ended in a terrible row.'

✣

He spent the morning signing paper after paper, until his arm finally gave up.

The ideal statue of a bureaucrat, he thought, should have its right arm in a sling.

He headed off for Marinella, thinking he would find Livia on the beach, sunbathing.

Instead he found her standing in the doorway of the house, all dressed up.

'I have to go back to Genoa immediately.'

'Why?'

'They phoned me from the office, and two of my colleagues have called in sick. I didn't have the heart to say no. You know how things are these days. They're always looking for the slightest excuse to get rid of you.'

Damn! Just when things were beginning to go so well between them.

'Have you already changed the ticket?'

'Yes, I'm on the five o'clock flight.'

Montalbano glanced at his watch. It was exactly one o'clock.

'Listen, we still have an hour at our disposal. I don't have anything pressing to do, so I can drive you to Palermo. We can go straight away and have a quick lunch at Enzo's, or we can . . .'

Livia smiled.

'Let's do the second thing . . .' she said.

✳

The drive to the airport went smoothly until they reached the junction at Lercara Freddi. Here the road was blocked, and a traffic policeman explained to Montalbano that two trucks had got wedged together, and they'd had to set up a detour.

All at once they found themselves on a sort of unmade road in the middle of an ocean of snapdragons with immensely tall wind turbines rising up at regular intervals.

Livia was spellbound.

'You certainly have some striking landscapes down here . . .'

'Why, don't you have any in Liguria?'

A polite exchange, showing that all was well between them. Otherwise the same landscape would have been 'crawling with bandits'.

*

They arrived at Punta Raisi airport an hour early, just in time to find out that the flight would be leaving an hour late.

Since they'd skipped lunch, Livia took advantage of the situation to stuff herself with cannoli.

When her plane finally took off, Montalbano phoned the station, informing Catarella that he would not be coming in that afternoon. He also rang Adelina to tell her that the coast was clear and that she could come back the following morning. To return to Vigàta, he went the long way, which passed through Fiacca. He got there around eight-thirty and headed straight for a restaurant that served langouste.

He had a feast.

By eleven he was home. He had barely set foot inside when the telephone rang.

It was Livia, who was very upset.

'Where on earth were you? I called four times! I thought you must have had an accident!'

He calmed her down, had a shower, and sat down on the veranda with cigarettes and whisky.

He didn't want to think about anything, just watch the sea in the night.

After about an hour of this, he went inside, turned on the television, and sat down in an armchair.

He was tuned in to TeleVigàta, which meant that the screen soon filled with the chicken-arsed face of Pippo Ragonese, their editor-in-chief, whose editorials followed one ironclad rule: they were always on the side of whoever was in power.

And he had it in for Montalbano.

'We've been informed, through unofficial channels, that a highly specialized, very well-organized gang of thieves has been at work in Vigàta over the past few days. Apparently a number of burglaries have taken place using an unusual technique that would be too complicated to explain in detail here. And supposedly the gang is not made up of foreigners, as is often the case, but of Sicilians. What is most surprising is the silence of the police on the matter.

'We do know, however, that the investigation is being

handled by Inspector Montalbano. In all honesty, we cannot say that it is in good hands, given the pre—'

Montalbano zapped the screen with the remote, telling him to fuck off.

One question lingered, however: how did Ragonese know about the burglaries? Surely nobody from the police department or the prosecutor's office could have told him.

Want to bet it was the gang's mastermind himself who informed him with an anonymous letter?

Pretentious as he was, it was possible he didn't like the fact that his deeds weren't making headlines.

Montalbano felt a little tired. Driving wore him out. He decided to go to bed.

And he had a dream.

*

Without knowing why or wherefore, he found himself in the middle of an arena, all dressed up like a paladin in the puppet theatre, on horseback, with his lance in rest.

A great many ladies and knights were watching the joust, and they were all standing, looking at him, and shouting:

'Hurrah for Salvo! Hurrah for Christendom's champion!'

Impeded in his movements by his armour, he couldn't reply with a bow, and so he raised his arm, which weighed a ton, and waved his steel-gloved hand.

Then the trumpets sounded and a knight clad entirely

in black armour entered the arena, a frightening giant of a man with his face hidden by his lowered visor.

Charlemagne himself stood up and said: 'Let the battle begin!'

And Montalbano immediately began to charge the black knight, who for his part remained as still as a statue.

Then, just like that, the black knight's lance struck his shoulder, knocking him off his horse.

As he was falling, the black knight raised his visor. He had no face. In its place was a sort of rubber ball. Then Montalbano realized that the faceless knight was the mastermind of the burglary ring, and was about to kill him.

Jesus Christ! He was going to look so bad in front of all those people!

He woke up in a sweat, his heart chugging wildly.

*

The phone rang shortly after eight.

He cursed the saints.

His secret intention had been to stay in bed until nine, so Adelina could bring him coffee in bed.

'Hello?' he said rudely into the receiver.

'*Matre santa*, Chief! I canna help it, bu' 'ere's been anutter buggery! If you wan', I c'n call back in a half a hour,' Catarella whined.

'What's done is done, Cat. Tell me about it.'

'Mrs Angelica Cosulicchio call juss now.'

Cosulicchio? Cosulich! Angelica Cosulich was number fourteen on the list.

QED.

'Where's she live?'

'On Via Cavurro, nummer fitteen.'

But that was the same street as the Peritores! 'Have you told Fazio?'

''E's toined off.'

'All right, call the lady back and tell her I'm on my way.'

✻

The building Miss Cosulich lived in was shaped like an ice-cream cone. Including the little bits of hazelnut sprinkled on top. 'Cosulich?' he asked the doorman.

'Which?'

Good God, he couldn't bear another spat with a doorman. He felt like turning on his heel and leaving, but he overcame the impulse.

'Cosulich.'

'I got that the first time; I'm not deaf. But there are two Cosuliches here. Angelica and Tripolina.'

He wanted to say Tripolina, just so he could meet a woman with such a strange name.

'Angelica.'

'Top floor.'

The lift was super-fast, practically punching him in the stomach as he soared up to the penthouse — that is, to the level of the whipped cream that usually crowns the ice-cream cone.

There was only one door on the entire enormous crescent-shaped landing, and the inspector rang the doorbell.

'Who is it?' a woman's voice asked moments later from inside the door.

'Inspector Montalbano.'

The door opened, and three things happened to the inspector, in the following order:

First, his vision clouded over slightly; second, his legs began to give way; and third, he was suddenly quite out of breath.

Because not only was Miss Cosulich a stunningly natural beauty of about thirty, without a hint of makeup, a rarity in this day of face-painted savages, but also . . .

Was it real, or was it all just his imagination?

Miss Cosulich looked exactly like, was the spitting image of, the figure of Angelica in Ariosto's *Orlando Furioso*, or at least the way he'd imagined her and pined for her, in the flesh, when, aged sixteen, he looked in secret at the illustrations by Gustave Doré, which his aunt had forbidden him to see.

It was inconceivable, a true miracle.

> *This knight, who now approached, at first glance*
> *Had recognized, though from afar, the one*
> *Who with angelic beauty unsurpassed*
> *In amorous enchantment held him fast.*

Angelica, oh Angelica!

He had fallen wildly in love with her, and lost a great deal of sleep almost every night, imagining that he was doing lewd things with her that he would never have had the courage to mention even to his closest friend.

Ah, how often he had imagined himself as Medoro, the shepherd Angelica fell in love with, driving poor Orlando so furiously mad!

He would picture to himself, sighing and trembling, the scene in the cave, where she lay naked on the straw, with a fire burning, as it rained outside and the sheep called in the distance, saying baaa baaaa . . .

More than a month that happy pair content

> *Remained and of their joy gave every proof.*
> *No further than his face her glances went.*
> *For his love she could not have enough.*
> *Unceasingly she hung upon his side,*
> *Yet her desire was never satisfied.*

'Please come in,' said Angelica Cosulich.

The light fog clouding his eyes lifted, and only then did Montalbano notice that she was wearing a form-fitting white blouse.

> *Like milky curds but freshly heaped within*
> *Their plaited moulds, her rounded breasts . . .*

Actually, those breasts were not Angelica's, but still . . .

SIX

'Please come in,' the young woman said again, starting to smile at Montalbano's obvious bewilderment.

Her smile was like a 100-watt light bulb suddenly coming on in a dark room.

It took a great effort of will for Montalbano to go from sixteen years of age to his current, miserable fifty-eight.

'Sorry, I was just thinking of something.' He went in.

Already from the entrance he got a sense of the damage the burglars had done in the apartment.

It was enormous, furnished in the latest style, and made you feel as though you were inside a spaceship. It must also have had a terrace without end. And circular, naturally.

'Listen,' said Angelica, 'the only room that's sort of liveable in at the moment is the kitchen. Do you mind if we go in there?'

I'd follow you even into a cold-storage room, Montalbano thought to himself.

But he said: 'Not at all.'

She was wearing a pair of skin-tight black trousers, and watching her walk from behind was a gift from God. And made him feel simultaneously stronger and weaker.

She pulled out a chair for him.

'Please sit down. Shall I make you some coffee?'

'Yes, thanks. But first I'd like a glass of water.'

'Are you feeling all right, Inspector?'

'I feel ex . . . excellent.' The water revived him.

Exactly the same thing had happened at the Peritores'. Except that there was no other man present now.

Actually, it seemed as if there was no trace of any man whatsoever in that apartment.

She poured the coffee, a cup for him and another for her, and then sat down facing him.

They drank in silence.

This was fine for Montalbano. In fact, they could sit there drinking coffee until the morning as far as he was concerned. Or, better yet, until they declared him a missing person at the police station.

Then she said:

'If you feel like smoking, go right ahead. In fact, why don't you offer me one while you're at it?'

She got up, went and found an ashtray, and sat down again.

Taking her first puff, she said in a soft voice:

'To cut a long story short, it was a carbon copy of the burglary of my friends the Peritores.'

Her voice was a celestial harmony, and it charmed him as the snake charmer's flute charms the python.

But he had to get down to work, damnit, even though he didn't feel like it at all. He cleared his throat, which was dry in spite of the water he had just drunk.

'Did you also spend the night in another house of yours, out of town?'

She had very long blonde hair which hung halfway down her back.

Before answering, she turned her face away. For the first time, she seemed a little ill at ease. 'Yes, but . . .'

'But?'

'It's not a house.'

'Is it an apartment?'

'Not even that.'

What, was she sleeping in a tent or a caravan? 'What is it, then?'

She took a long drag, blew out the smoke, then looked the inspector in the eye.

'It's a bedroom with a double bed, and a bathroom. With a separate entrance. Know what I mean?'

A shot straight to the heart, direct, precise. Fired by an expert markswoman. It hurt, but

A flood of sorrow in his bosom stays,
And by its very impetus is checked . . .

'I see,' he said.

A pied-à-terre. Also called a love nest in common parlance. But it was the first time he'd ever met a woman who had one.

He felt a sudden pang of irrational jealousy, like Orlando when

He sees Angelica and Medoro
Intertwined a hundred times . . .

She explained:

'I have a boyfriend, but he works abroad and only comes to Italy once a year, and so, every now and then, I need . . . Please try and understand. It's not a steady thing with anybody.'

Can I get on the waiting list? he wanted to ask, but said only:

'Tell me what happened.'

'Well, last night, after dinner – it must have been around nine-thirty – I got in my car and headed for Montelusa. Just outside town, I picked up the . . . man I had an appointment with and drove to the villa where I rent the room.'

'Excuse me for interrupting, but who owns the villa?'

'A cousin of mine who lives in Milan and only comes for a fortnight in the summer.'

'Excuse me for interrupting again . . .'

'It's your job,' Angelica said, smiling.

Love nest or not, it was the sort of thing to be eaten slowly, in small bites, like a succulent fruit.

'Did the burglars rifle through your room as well?'

'Of course.'

'What about the villa itself?'

'Well, I had the same question, and so I went to look. I know where the keys are kept. No, they didn't enter the villa.'

'Go on.'

'There's not much more to say. We had a drink, talked as best we could, and then went to bed.'

> And every time his heart in his chest
> Leapt as though gripped by an icy hand.

'I'm sorry, I don't want to . . .'

'Not at all, go ahead.'

'You said you talked as best you could.'

'Yes, and so?'

'What do you mean?'

'Well, it's not as if the boys I go with have to be cultured or anything. I'm interested in other talents. The one yesterday was practically half illiterate.'

Montalbano gulped. It tasted bitter. How did that other poet put it?

> a fisher of sponges
> will win this rare pearl . . .

'Go on.'

'What else is there? I woke up at seven with the worst headache. Whereas he was still out like a light. When I reached over to the bedside table for my watch, which I'd left there, it was gone. I thought it must have fallen off, so I got up, and only then did I realize I'd been robbed of everything.'

'Everything meaning what?'

'My watch, my necklace, my bracelet, mobile phone, computer, purse, handbag, and the keys to this apartment. Then I went outside, and the car was also gone.'

'Why had you brought your computer with you?'

'Pertinent question,' she said, laughing. 'To watch a few educational videos, know what I mean?'

> *Of all his hopes, Orlando, not to show*
> *His grief, all signs of it attempts to check . . .*

'Yes. How did you get home?'

'My cousin keeps a runabout in the garage for when he's here.'

'Did you have a lot of money in your purse?'

'Three thousand euros.'

'Go on.'

'I raced home, knowing what I would find there.'

'Did they take a lot of stuff?'

'A lot. And very valuable stuff, unfortunately.'

'You'll have to come to headquarters and make a statement.'

'I'll come later this morning. I have to work out exactly what they took.'

She paused.

'Could I have another cigarette?'

Montalbano lit it for her.

'So why aren't you doing what you're supposed to do?' she asked out of the blue.

Montalbano balked.

'Why? What am I supposed to do?'

'I don't know, pull out a magnifying glass, take some pictures, call the Forensics lab . . .'

'For fingerprints, you mean?'

'Well, yes.'

'Do you really think that burglars as skilled as these wouldn't wear gloves? No, no, it would be a waste of time. Speaking of which, how did they get into your lo— your room?'

He'd very nearly said 'love nest', which would have been a terrible gaffe.

But why a gaffe, really? Angelica was a woman who didn't mince words. She called a spade a spade.

'My room is located at the back of the villa, and you reach it by an external staircase. Next to the entrance there's a window with a grating. It's more or less the only ventilation, and so I left it open. Aside from the bed, there's also a little table, of course, with two chairs. I always leave the keys to the room on the table. The thieves must have pumped the gas in through the window, which they must have then shut. Then, after the gas took effect, they opened it again, and using a telescopic pole with a hook at the end, they pulled the table closer to themselves, so all they had to do was reach out and grab the keys.'

Specialists in telescopic poles, first with a magnet, and now with a hook . . .

'Excuse me, but this business of the pole with the hook . . . How do you know this? Was this your surmise?'

'No, no, I saw it; I saw the pole. They left it there.' Montalbano closed his eyes for a moment. Now came the most painful part for him. He took a deep breath and dived in.

'I have to ask you a couple of personal questions,' he said.

'Go ahead.'

'Have you ever brought the same man to your room more than once?'

'Never. I don't like reheated soup.'

'How often do you use it?'

'Definitely once every couple of weeks. Of course there are exceptions, sometimes.'

I am not, am not what I seem to be . . .

'Of course,' said Montalbano, with seeming indifference.

Then he asked:

'Have you ever had, I dunno, have you ever quarrelled with any of them?'

'Once.'

'When?'

'About a month ago.'

'May I ask what it was about?'

'He wanted more.'

'How much had you agreed on?'

'Two thousand.'

'And how much did he want?'

'Four.'

'Did you give it to him?'

'No.'

'How did you get out of it?'

'I threatened him.'

'How?'

'With a gun.'

She said it as though aiming a gun at someone was the most natural thing in the world.

'Are you kidding?'

'Absolutely not. When I go there with someone, I feel a lot safer if I have my gun with me. I have a licence for it.'

Unlike the Angelica of his youth, this one didn't flee from danger.

Montalbano recovered from a light swoon.

'And did you have your gun with you last night?'

'Yes.'

'And did they steal that too?'

'Of course.'

'Listen, this is very serious. When you come to head-quarters, be sure to bring all the relevant documents concerning this weapon.'

'OK.'

'I'm sorry, but do you have a job?'

'Yes.'

'What kind of a job?'

'I'm chief cashier at the Banca Siculo-Americana. I've been working there for the last six months or so.'

Maybe I should transfer my account there, he thought.

But he asked instead:

'Can you explain to me how you find the men you go with?'

'Well, I dunno, chance encounters, bank clients . . . You know, sometimes there's not even any need to talk; there's an immediate understanding.'

'Listen, the keys to this place . . .'

'I left them in the entranceway.'

'One more question. Where are you from?'

'I was born in Trieste. But my mother was from Vigàta.'

'She's no longer around?'

'No. Nor is my father. There was a terrible . . . accident here. I was only five at the time. I wasn't here when it happened; my parents had sent me to my grandparents' place, in Trieste.'

Her blue eyes had turned darker. Apparently the death of her parents was still a painful subject for her.

Montalbano stood up. She did likewise.

'I need to ask you a very big favour,' Angelica said, letting her hair cover her face.

'Go right ahead.'

'Could we leave out the first part?'

'I'm sorry, I don't think I understand.'

She took a step forward and put her hands on his lapels. She was standing very close to him, and Montalbano could smell the scent of her skin. It made him dizzy.

It felt as if her hands were on fire. Surely they would leave burned handprints on his jacket when she removed them.

'Could you . . . find a way not to bring up this business of the room, and say that only this place was robbed?'

Montalbano felt in danger of melting like an ice cream in the sun.

'Well, it would be possible . . . but illegal.'

'So you really can't?'

'I could, but . . . what's to stop the man you spent the night with going around telling everyone what really happened?'

'You would have to take care of that yourself.'

She removed her hands from his lapels, let them

wander up to his shoulders, then folded them behind his neck.

From this position, her lips were dangerously close to his.

The more he seeks to find a lasting peace,
The more he finds just suffering and pain.

'If anyone found out about this room, you see, I would be ruined, you understand. I've been sincere with you. I realized at once that I could trust you . . . But if word were ever to get out, there would certainly be repercussions at the bank. I might even get fired . . . Oh, please! I would be so grateful!'

Montalbano quickly freed himself, unlinking her hands and taking a step back.

'I'll see what I can do. I'll see you later.' He practically ran away.

He was all sweaty and felt as numb as if he had drunk half a bottle of whisky.

*

He told the whole story to Fazio. Naturally, he said nothing of how he had felt about Angelica.

'Let's take one thing at a time, Chief. Let's start with the burglary of the love nest.'

For whatever reason, Fazio's choice of terms bothered him.

'Do you have any idea why they leave behind the special tools they use to break into people's apartments?' Fazio continued.

'The telescopic poles? I've been thinking a lot about that. These people don't do anything without a reason. First of all, it's a sort of bank shot that keeps being repeated in exactly the same way.'

'I don't understand.'

'I'll explain. The robbery always takes place in two phases. First they go into a house, a bedroom, wherever you like, when the owner is asleep inside. And they do this because they need the keys to the other residence, the apartment in town. And so they bank the shot off rail A so that the ball will come back and hit rail B. Is that any clearer?'

'Absolutely.'

'This is how I realized that the burglary of Incardona's country house was a red herring. It didn't correspond with their modus operandi.'

'And what about the tools?'

'I was getting to that. Leaving them at the scene of the crime means two things. It must be an idea of the master-mind's. One the one hand, it means that they won't be returning, and on the other, it's a way for the leader to tell us that he's got more tricks up his sleeve. That he can always come up with other ways of getting his hands on a set of keys. The same as leaving the keys in the entrance hall of the burgled apartments. He's saying: "We don't need these any more." Make sense to you?'

'Makes sense to me. But what do you think about the fact that Miss Cosulich doesn't want us to say anything about her love nest?'

'I'm in two minds about that. On the one hand, I'd like to do her that favour, and on the other hand, I'm afraid the man she was with . . .'

'There's a remedy for that,' said Fazio. 'When Miss Cosulich comes in to make her statement, I'll ask her what his name is, and then I'll go and talk to him. I'll convince him to be as quiet as a fish.'

'But he's not the only problem.'

'What do you mean?'

'I mean that the fact that we've filed a report that doesn't correspond with reality will also be known by the brains of the gang, who we'll call Mr Z. And he could use this illegal omission against us at any time.'

'That's to be expected,' said Fazio. 'But as you yourself pointed out, Mr Z is a pretentious man.'

'So?'

'Maybe such an omission will bother him and he'll make a false move. What do you think?'

Montalbano didn't answer. 'Chief, did you hear me?'

Montalbano was staring at the wall in front of him. Fazio was worried.

'You feeling all right, Chief?'

SEVEN

Montalbano shot to his feet and slapped himself on the forehead.

'What an idiot I am! You're right. We'll write the report the way La Cosulich wants. But you must do something for me right away.'

'What?'

'Take the list of the Peritores' friends and check to see which have second homes where they spend weekends or go and sleep every so often. We'll meet in an hour or so.'

'But where are you going?'

'I'm going to see Zito.'

Going to Montelusa meant he might miss his chance to see Angelica again, but such was life.

*

He pulled up outside the Free Channel studios, got out of the car, and went in. The secretary flashed him a big smile.

'What a lovely surprise! Long time no see! You're looking good, Inspector.'

'And you're more beautiful every time I see you.'

'The boss is in his office. You can go right in.'

He and Zito were friends from way back.

The door to the newsman's office was open, and Zito, upon seeing him, got up and came forward to embrace him.

'How's the wife and kid?' Montalbano asked.

'Everyone's fine. You need something?'

'Yeah.'

'At your service.'

'Did you hear Ragonese's report on the two burglaries?'

'Yes.'

'Well, there's been a third. But nobody knows about it yet.'

'So you're giving me the scoop exclusively?'

'Yeah.'

'Thanks. What do you want me to say?'

'That there was a robbery at the apartment of Miss Angelica Cosulich, who lives in Vigàta at Via Cavour 15. You should point out that there'd already been a burglary at number 13 on the same street, at the home of the Peritores. Also mention that Miss Cosulich was at home asleep at the time of the robbery, but was rendered unconscious by knockout gas. And there you have it.'

'What are you hoping to gain by this?'

'A reaction.'

'On whose part?'

'I don't know, to be honest. But if you receive an anonymous phone call or letter concerning the story, let me know at once. I mean it.'

'I'll feature it on the I p.m. report,' said Zito. 'Then I'll run it again on the evening news.'

*

Montalbano drove back to headquarters at 70 kph, which for him was Formula I–level speed.

'Get me Fazio,' he said to Catarella.

'Chief,' Fazio said when he came in, 'I did what you wanted with just a few phone calls. Of the people on the list, there are two couples and one single person who have a house outside of town: the Sciortinos, the Pintacudas, and Mr Maniace, who's a widower.'

'Did you find out where these houses are located?'

'Yes, I got the addresses.'

'All right, now we need these people to tell us when they plan to—'

'Already taken care of,' said Fazio. 'I worked out where you were going with this, so I took the liberty of—'

'You were absolutely right. Clearly the final break-in will be in one of these three houses.'

'Mr Sciortino told me that a couple of friends from Rome may be arriving today. And they'll all go to their seaside house. They agreed to let me know if and when they do.'

'And has Miss Cosulich turned up?'

'Not yet.'

'By the way, the widow Cannavò, the busybody – did she tell you anything about La Cosulich?'

'Are you kidding? She built her a monument! A statue to put on the altar! She told me the girl is faithful to the end to her boyfriend, who comes to see her only once a year, and that she's always got a pack of men running around her, but she stands fast! A fortress, she is.'

Montalbano smiled.

'I guess La Cosulich has successfully kept her love nest a secret! Which is why she doesn't want anyone finding out now.'

He glanced at his watch. It was almost one. The telephone rang.

It was Angelica.

'Sorry I'm late. I'm on my way now.'

'When you get here, ask for Inspector Fazio. He'll take your statement.'

'Oh.'

Her tone seemed slightly disappointed. Or was he wrong?

'So I won't be seeing you? I'd thought . . . that, well, if you weren't already engaged, we could have lunch.'

A wound far deeper and broader is made
In the heart by a sharp arrow unseen.

'Just come to my office after you're finished with Fazio,' Montalbano said in a tone halfway between bureaucratic and indifferent.

Whereas if Fazio hadn't been still there in his room, he would have started jumping for joy.

✢

How was he going to make the time pass while Angelica was giving her statement to Fazio?

The question called to mind an episode when he was deputy inspector. The thought of it slightly lessened the agitation that had come over him and was making him tingle inside.

One night he was sent on a stakeout with two other men in a dark alley in a village he didn't know, some thirty-odd houses lost in the mountains.

They were hoping to catch a fugitive.

They waited all night, and then the sun rose.

There was nothing more for them to do. The operation had been a failure.

And so he went with his men to have some coffee and noticed, in the distance, a little shop with newspapers on display.

He walked over to it, but when he reached that strange

sort of news-stand, he noticed that the newspapers on display were old, dating back to 1940.

There was even a copy of *Il Popolo d'Italia*, the pre-eminent Fascist newspaper, with Mussolini's speech declaring war on the front page.

Puzzled and curious, he went into the shop.

On the dust-covered shelves inside there were bars of soap, tubes of toothpaste, razor blades, boxes of brilliantine, all from the same period as the newspapers.

Behind the counter was a very thin man of about seventy, with a goatee and thick glasses.

'I'd like some toothpaste, please,' said Montalbano.

The old man handed him a tube.

'You'd better try it first,' he advised. 'It might not be good any more.'

Montalbano unscrewed the cap, squeezed it, and instead of the usual little worm of paste, what came out was a sort of pink dust.

'It's all dried up,' the old man said disconsolately.

But Montalbano's eyes lit up with a flash of amusement.

'Let's try another,' he said, curious to get to the bottom of this mystery.

The second tube likewise contained only dust. 'Forgive me for asking,' said Montalbano, 'but can you tell me what you get out of keeping a shop like this?'

'What I get, sir? I get to pass the time with outsiders like you.'

And making the time pass meant surviving.

Like the time he competed with a lizard in resisting the sun . . .

✻

There was a knock at the door. 'Come in.'

It was Fazio and Angelica.

'It didn't take long because the young lady was very thorough. She brought us a very detailed list of everything that was stolen,' said Fazio.

'So we can go now?' Montalbano asked Angelica.

'The sooner the better,' she replied, smiling.

✻

'Do you have a car?'

'Have you forgotten they stole it?'

With her walking so close beside him, he was no longer all there in the head.

'Then we'll go in mine.'

'Where are you taking me?'

'Where I usually go. Enzo's. Have you ever eaten there?'

'No. We have an arrangement with a little restaurant behind the bank. It's only so-so. Is Enzo's good?'

'Excellent. Otherwise I wouldn't go there.'

'I like good food too. Nothing fancy, just simple, good stuff.'

A point in her favour.

Actually the thousand-and-first point in her favour, considering the first thousand she'd already won just by her presence.

Enzo, too, was struck by the young woman's beauty, and he didn't hide it. He stood there mildly spellbound, looking at her slack-jawed. Then, when he noticed an imperceptible little spot on the tablecloth, he insisted on changing it.

'What'll you have?'

'I'll have whatever the gentleman is having,' said Angelica.

She felt her heart invaded bit by bit
Till burning passion had encompassed it.

Montalbano began the litany. 'Seafood antipasto?'

'Good!'

'Spaghetti with sea-urchin sauce?'

'Excellent!'

'Fried mullet?'

'Perfect!'

'The house white?'

'All right.'

Enzo walked away happy.

Now came the hard thing to talk about.

'You'll probably think me rude, and rightly so, but I have to warn you. I really don't like to talk when I'm eating. But since it's you, I will gladly listen if you want to speak.'

Angelica started laughing.

A laughter made of pearls falling to the floor and bouncing, falling back down and bouncing back up again.

An elderly patron of the restaurant, sitting alone, turned towards Angelica and bowed in homage to her.

'Why are you laughing?'

'Because I don't like to talk when I'm eating, either. You can imagine how unbearable it is to sit at a table with colleagues talking about nothing but work!'

They didn't exchange another word. Only glances, smiles, hums, and affirmations, in great quantity.

It was much better than a long conversation.

They took things easy, and when they finally left the trattoria, they felt a little weighted down.

'Shall I take you home?'

'Are you going back to headquarters?'

'Not right away. First . . .'

'What are you going to do?'

'Well . . .'

Should he tell her or not? Could he ever keep anything secret from her?

'I'm going to drive to the harbour, park, and take a walk along the eastern jetty, out to the lighthouse, where I'm going to sit down on a rock and smoke a cigarette. Then I'll go back to the office.'

'Is there room for two on this rock?'

*

There was room, but not much, and thus their bodies were in continuous contact.

An ever-so-light breeze was blowing.

> *For love, who burns my heart within my breast,*
> *Fanning it with his wings, creates this breeze.*

They finished their cigarettes without saying a word. Then she said:

'About that favour I asked of you . . .'

'Fazio didn't say anything to you?'

'No.'

'We decided to comply with your request.'

In reply to your question, he should have said first, if he really wanted to play the perfect bureaucrat.

He realized that they were both balancing their words as on a gymnast's beam; one too many or too few might spoil the whole situation.

'Thanks,' she said.

'Shall we go back?' Montalbano asked.

'Let's go back.'

How naturally and simply Angelica took his hand in hers on the walk back!

*

They returned to the car.

'Shall I give you a lift to the bank?'

'No. I asked for the day off. I want to put everything back in order at home. My cleaning lady's coming to help.'

'So I'll take you home instead?'

'I'd rather walk. It's not so far, really. But thanks for the company.'

'Thank you.'

*

In the days that followed, he couldn't remember how he'd spent that afternoon at the office.

Surely Fazio came to talk to him about something, but damned if he understood the first thing of any of it.

His body sat in the chair behind the desk; this was verified by all who saw it. But what they didn't see was that his head had become detached from his body and was stuck to the ceiling like a child's helium balloon.

He said Yes, yes and No, no at the right times and the wrong times.

Fazio came in a second time, saw him with a faraway look in his eyes, and decided to go back to where he'd come from.

The inspector felt a little feverish.

Why didn't Angelica find some excuse and give him a ring? He needed to hear her voice.

Ah, cruel Love! What is the reason why
You seldom make our longings correspond?

At last it was eight o'clock. Time to go home to Marinella.

He stood up, went out of his office, and when he was passing Catarella, he asked:

'Were there any phone calls for me?'

'Nah, Chief, not f' yiz.'

'Are you sure?'

'Assolutely.'

'Well, have a good—'

'Acktchully, Chief,' Catarella interrupted him, 'jess now there 'uz a general callin' 'at called.'

'You mean a general in the army or something?'

'Nah, Chief, general inna sense 'at i'z about sumpin' generally general.'

What could it mean?

'Could you be a little clearer?'

'Twuz a ginnelman 'oo din't want nuttin' in pattickler.'

'But what did he say?'

'Sumpin' useless 'atta police can't do nuttin' wit' noways.'

'Just tell me anyway.'

'I didna unnastann' much, Chief. 'E said as how since 'is frenn arrived, 'e was gonna leave. So wha' was I asposta say? I jess wisht 'im a nice holiday.'

A thought exploded in Montalbano's head like a thunderbolt.

'Did he say what his name was?'

'Yessir, 'e did, an' I writ it down.' Catarella picked up a scrap of paper. 'Sciocchino, 'e said 'is name was.'

Sciortino! Who, as they'd arranged, was supposed to inform him when he went to his house by the sea!

'Call Fazio and tell him to come to my office at once.'

He went back to his room, and Fazio arrived a minute later.

'What's up, Chief?'

'The Sciortinos have gone to the seaside with their friends from Rome. I worked it out by piecing together what Catarella told me. I almost missed it. It's our fault; we forgot to warn him.'

'Damn! I already sent Gallo home!'

'We'll send someone else.'

'Chief, we're short on personnel. With all these cuts the government keeps making . . .'

'And they have the audacity to call it a law for public safety! We've got no cars, no petrol, no guns, no men . . . It's clear they're determined to promote criminality. Enough. What can we do?'

'If you want, I'll go myself,' said Fazio.

There was only one solution. Montalbano weighed the pros and cons and arrived at his conclusion.

'Listen, let's do this. I'll go home, eat dinner, and then around eleven I'll go and stand guard. Then you'll come and relieve me around three in the morning. Give me the address of this house.'

As he was driving home, it occurred to him that it might be best, while it was still light outside, to go and have a look at the Sciortinos' seaside house, which was about six miles down the coast from his place, past Punta Bianca.

It turned out to be a good idea.

Right behind the house, which was almost on the beach, was a small hill with a few trees. One reached it by way of the provincial road.

Parking at the side of the road, he could keep an eye on the whole situation while remaining comfortably seated in his car.

He headed home.

As often happened, he heard the phone ringing just as he was opening the front door. He managed to pick it up in time.

It was Livia.

He didn't want to admit to himself that he was slightly disappointed.

Livia informed him that she was calling now because she was going to be out late at a meeting with the unions.

'And since when do you have anything to do with the unions?'

'I was picked by my colleagues to do it. Unfortunately the company's planning some redundancies.'

Montalbano wished her luck.

He went and opened the fridge. Nothing. He opened the oven and rejoiced.

Adelina had prepared a plateful of aubergine *parmigiana* that would have fed four. It smelled perfect.

He laid the table on the veranda and started eating, utterly thrilled.

Since, after eating, he still had an hour or so to go, he took a shower and put on an old but comfortable suit.

He heard the phone ring and went to answer. It was Angelica.

His heart started chugging like an old train going uphill.

EIGHT

'Why are you panting?'

'I was just jogging.'

'I phoned the station and they were kind enough to give me your home number.'

Pause.

'I just wanted to wish you good night.' It was suddenly springtime.

Daisies popping out of the spaces between the tiles in the floor.

Two swallows alighted on top of the bookcase and started twittering (if that's what swallows actually do).

'Thanks. Unfortunately it won't be a good night.' Why did he say it?

Did he want her to feel sorry for him, or did he want her to see him as a warrior, like Orlando?

'Why not?'

'I have to keep watch over the Sciortinos' house.'

'I know where it is. Do you think the burglars . . .
tonight . . . ?'

'It's fairly likely.'

'Will you be going alone?'

'Yes.'

'And where will you hide?'

'You know that little hill behind the—'

'Oh, I get it . . .'

Another pause.

'Well, good night anyway, and good luck.'

'You too.'

So she did call, in the end! Better than nothing. He
headed towards his car, singing, 'Guarda come dondolo . . .'

*

After sitting in the car on the hill for about ten minutes,
he realized it wasn't such a good idea.

The Sciortinos and their friends had made a barbecue
on the beach and were now smoking and drinking.

Therefore there was no need for his surveillance. He
could let himself think a little.

This was a big mistake.

Because he didn't think at all about the investigation,
the burglars, or Mr Z.

He thought about Angelica.

> And thus so deep in thought he has now gone,
> It is as though he has turned into stone.

Sitting there motionless, he began to feel an overwhelming sense of shame rise up inside him.

Though there was nobody there with him, he felt his cheeks burning red from the embarrassment.

What had he done? Had he lost his mind?

Carrying on with that girl as if he was some lovestruck sixteen-year-old! It was one thing to languish over a drawing of a woman at sixteen, and another thing entirely to start acting the fool with a real girl in the flesh.

He had confused his boyhood dream with his reality as a man of nearly sixty.

Ridiculous! That's what he was, a ridiculous man! Falling head over heels with a girl who could be his daughter!

What did he hope to get out of it?

Angelica had been a fantasy of his youth, and now he wanted to cling, with her help, to a youth long gone?

An old codger's pipe dreams, that's what these were! He had to break things off at once.

It was beneath the dignity of a man like him.

And it was likely Fazio knew exactly what was going on and was laughing at him.

What a wretched, contemptible spectacle he was making of himself!

More than an hour he passed in thought, head bowed . . .

No! Enough of this *Orlando Furioso* crap!

Despite the fact that the windows were open, he gasped for air inside the car.

He opened the door, got out, took a few steps around. He could hear the four people on the beach laughing.

He lit a cigarette and noticed that his hands were shaking.

They couldn't see him from down below.

At any rate, as a preliminary measure, he would unplug the phone as soon as he got home. Just in case Angelica got it into her head to call him in the middle of the night.

Then, tomorrow morning, as soon as he got to work, he would order Catarella to . . .

He suddenly noticed a car turning off the main road. It extinguished its headlights and continued slowly in the darkness, with the engine running silently, towards the spot where he was parked.

His heart leapt into his throat. It was surely the thieves.

They, too, had chosen the hill as their observation point.

He tossed aside his cigarette and, bent over, hurried back to his car, opened the glove compartment, took his gun, and crouched down.

The car advanced slowly, headlights still off. He formulated a plan.

Arresting them now made no sense; in fact, it would be a big mistake.

He had to wait for them to try to break in to the house. At which point he would immediately call the Sciortinos on his mobile and alert them. They would start yelling and shouting for help, and the frightened robbers would abandon their efforts.

He, meanwhile, would make sure that when the thieves turned tail and got back in their car, they would find it out of order.

The rest he would improvise.

The car stopped a short distance away. The door opened. Out stepped Angelica.

> *With sweet and amorous affection filled,*
> *His goddess he approached without delay.*
> *She, with her arms about him, cooed and billed . . .*

Much later, after the Sciortinos and their friends had gone to bed, and the lights in the house were all out, and the full moon lit up the night like the day, he asked her:

'Why did you come?'

'For three reasons,' she said. 'Because I wasn't sleepy, because I wanted to see you again, and because I thought we would be less likely to arouse the burglars' suspicions if we were a couple kissing in the car.'

'Whose car did you come in?'

'I rented it this afternoon. I can't do without it.'

✳

'I don't like sitting in the car. We have time.'

'I don't like it either.'

*

Still later, around two-thirty in the morning, Montalbano told the girl that Fazio would be coming soon to relieve him.

'Do you want me to go?'

'I think it would be better.'

'Shall we have lunch tomorrow?'

'Ring me at the office. If I'm free . . .' They embraced and held each other tight.

Then they kissed for so long that they both came out of it panting, as if they had been holding their breaths underwater.

Then she left.

*

About ten minutes later, Fazio arrived. Montalbano was waiting for him at his car.

He didn't want Fazio to get too close. He smelled too much like Angelica.

'Any news?' asked Fazio.

Hell yes, there was news! An unexpected, divine miracle had happened. But it had nothing to do with the investigation.

'Nah. All quiet.'

For no reason at all, Fazio shone his big standard-issue police torch in the inspector's face.

'Chief! What happened to your lips?'

'Nothing, why?'

'They're all red and swollen.'

'Probably got a few mosquito bites.'

For almost four hours, he and Angelica had hardly done anything but embrace and kiss wildly.

'All right then, Chief, good night.'

'Good night to you too. Oh, and don't forget, don't hesitate to call me if you need anything.'

'All right.'

*

He knew there was no point in going to bed. He would have done nothing but toss and turn between the sheets, not sleeping a wink and thinking only of Angelica.

So he set himself up on the veranda, with cigarettes and whisky within reach. And he ended up watching the sun rise.

The usual solitary fisherman passed by, greeting him with a wave of the hand. Then he put his boat into the water.

'Want to come for a ride?'

'Why not? I'll be there in a minute.'

He went inside, put on his trunks, ran down to the

beach, stepped into the water, and climbed aboard the boat.

When they were out at sea, he dived in and went for a long swim, until he felt thoroughly exhausted.

The water was freezing cold, but it was what he needed to chill his blood, which had reached boiling point that night.

*

He showed up at the station all clean and shiny, and it wasn't even nine o'clock yet.

'Jeezis, Chief! Yer soitanly lookin' good dis mornin'! Ya look ten years younger!' Catarella exclaimed upon seeing him.

'Actually, Cat, if you'd said thirty years younger, that would have been even better,' Montalbano replied.

Then he asked: 'Any sign of Fazio?'

''E jess got in.'

'Send him to me.'

'All quiet,' said Fazio when he came in. 'I left at half-past five. Too late for burglars.'

'Maybe you ought to give the Sciortinos a ring and find out how long they plan to stay at Punta Bianca.'

'Already taken care of.'

Whenever Fazio said 'already taken care of', which he did often, it got on Montalbano's nerves.

'They're leaving the day after tomorrow,' Fazio continued.

'Which means that we have to organize shifts for tonight and tomorrow night as well.'

'Already taken care of.'

Under the desk, Montalbano's foot, on its own initiative, started tapping its heel against the floor.

'Will you be needing me?' he asked.

'No, Chief. For the time being you're off the hook. Unless you enjoy it . . .'

What was that supposed to mean?

Was Fazio insinuating something? Had he suspected anything?

Fazio was a redoubtable cop, and in such situations one had to take as many precautions as against the plague. 'How could I possibly enjoy staying awake in a car in the middle of the night?' Montalbano asked gruffly, on purpose.

Fazio said nothing.

'With all those mosquitoes that don't give you a moment's rest?' Montalbano continued.

'I didn't get a single bite,' said Fazio.

This time Montalbano said nothing. But he was hoping Angelica didn't call while Fazio was still in his office.

Suddenly, he had an idea.

He had the phone number of the Sciortinos' beach

house in his mobile, but he'd left it at home. He asked Fazio for it, then dialled it at once.

'Hello?' said a woman's voice.

'Good morning. Inspector Montalbano here. I'd like to speak to Mr Sciortino.'

'I'm his wife. I'll get him at once.'

'Good morning, Inspector, what can I do for you?'

'Mr Sciortino, I'm sorry to bother you, but I need some information.'

'I'm glad to help.'

'Did you tell your friends in Vigàta that you'd be going to your house by the sea for three days?'

'I'm sorry, but why do you ask?'

'I'm afraid I can't tell you, believe me.'

'I trust all my friends implicitly.'

'And I'm sure you have every reason to do so.'

'Anyway, it seems nothing happened last night, right?'

'Absolutely. But I want you please to answer me just the same.'

'I don't think I told anyone.'

'Think it over carefully.'

'No, nobody, I'm sure of it.'

'What about your wife?'

'Wait just a second.'

It really took him only a second. 'Antonietta says the same thing.'

'Well, thank you, then. You're very kind.'

As soon as he put down the receiver, Fazio said: 'That road leads nowhere, Chief.'

'What do you mean?'

'I realized what you were getting at. But even if the burglars don't turn up the next two nights, that doesn't mean Mr Z is one of the Peritores' eighteen friends. It's possible that Mr Z isn't part of that circle, or maybe he is but he has no interest in robbing the Sciortinos.'

'Good point,' Montalbano admitted.

Had he been in normal condition, he would never have thought of anything so stupid. And a man of nearly sixty besotted with a woman barely thirty could hardly be said to be in normal condition, could he?

More to appear nonchalant in front of Fazio than because of any real necessity, he phoned the Free Channel studios.

'Hello, this is Montalbano. Is Zito there?'

'Just a moment.'

The receiver started playing a passage from Wagner's *Ring of the Nibelung*, which was scarcely phone entertainment stuff.

'*Ciao*, Salvo.'

'*Ciao*. Listen, after you broadcast the news of the burglary, did you receive any reactions?'

'None. I would have called you in that case.'

'OK, bye.'

Another dead end, just to use another cliché. They looked at each other disconsolately.

'I'm going back to my office,' said Fazio, getting up and leaving.

Immediately afterwards, the telephone rang. 'Chief, iss Mrs Cosulicchio wants a talk t'yiz.'

'Is she here?'

'No, Chief, she's onna line.'

'Put her on.'

Perfect timing. 'Hi.'

'Hi.'

'Sleep well?' she asked.

'I didn't go to bed.'

'Were there any complications?'

'No. I just knew that I wouldn't be able to fall asleep, so I waited for the sun to rise.'

'I on the other hand slept like a rock. I'm calling from the office; I haven't got much time. I can't meet you for lunch.'

His heart crashed to the floor and most certainly suffered some injury.

'Why not?'

'I have to stay at the bank for about half an hour after closing. It wouldn't leave us much time.'

'Still better than nothing.'

'I don't agree. I get off work at six. I'll go home, change, and then come to your place, if that's all right and if you're free. That way we can go out to dinner instead of lunch.'

'All right.'

'Explain to me how to get to your house.'

The injuries to his heart miraculously healed.

*

He went to Enzo's for lunch.

'And where's the beautiful girl from yesterday?' Enzo seemed disappointed.

'She's just a chance acquaintance, Enzo.'

'I wish I could have the same chance as you.'

'What've you got for me?' said Montalbano, changing the subject.

'Whatever you like.'

The inevitable antipasto. Risotto with an assortment of fish. Two big fillets of sole that hung over the edge of the plate.

When the inspector was getting up to leave, Enzo called him.

'Telephone, Inspector.'

Who on earth had the nerve to bother him during lunch at the restaurant? There were strict standing orders against it.

'Beckin' yer partin', Chief, but hizzoner the c'mishner jess called madder 'n a tchaguar in a topical forest! Jeezis, was 'e ivver mad! Made the 'airs on my arms stann' up!'

'Wha'd he want?'

''E din't say. Bu' 'e's gonna call back in a haff a hour an' 'e says 'e assolutely wants yiz to be inna office assolutely to get 'is call!'

'All right, I'm on my way.'

So much for his walk along the jetty. How was he ever going to digest properly?

Better look for another solution.

'Enzo, bring me a *digestivo*, would you?'

'I've got some limoncello my wife made that's better than a plunger.'

And indeed it had a certain effect.

*

He'd been sitting at his desk for about ten minutes when the telephone rang.

'Iss him, Chief!' said Catarella, all agitated.

'Put him on.'

'Montalbano!'

'I'm here, Mr Commissioner.'

'Montalbano!'

'I'm still here, Mr Commissioner.'

'And that's my undoing! That you're still here instead of going to the devil! Instead of disappearing! But this time, as God is my witness, you're going to pay for this, and for all the other times!'

'I don't understand.'

'You will. I'll expect you at six p.m.'

Like hell you will! Not at six or any time thereafter, not even if God came down from heaven! He had to invent an excuse.

'At six, you say?'

'Yes. Are you going deaf?'

'But the *Pinkerton* is arriving at six!'

'What's that?'

'It's a ship, Mr Commissioner.'

NINE

'A ship? And what's that got to do with you?'

'The port authorities alerted me. Apparently there's contraband aboard.'

'But isn't that the job of the Customs Police?'

'Yes, sir, indeed it is. But they're all ill. There's a little stomach-bug epidemic. Apparently the drinking water got tainted.'

How many more lies could he come up with?

'Send your second-in-command!'

'He was let go, Mr Commissioner.'

'Let go? What the hell are you saying?'

'I'm sorry, I got that mixed up. I meant he's on a leave of absence.'

Damn Catarella!

'Then I'll expect you at five o'clock on the dot.' He hung up without saying goodbye.

What on earth could have happened? The telephone rang. It was Zito.

'Did you see Ragonese's editorial on the midday report?'

'No. What did he say?'

'Come over and I'll let you see the videotape. You need to hear this for yourself.'

Twenty minutes later he was rushing into the Free Channel studios.

'Let's go to the viewing room. It's all set up,' said Zito.

There wasn't anyone else there. Zito turned on the tape.

The pursed-lipped mouth on Ragonese's chicken-arse face began to speak.

'A very strange fact of unprecedented gravity has come to our attention. We will, of course, duly forward to Montelusa police commissioner Bonetti-Alderighi the letter that informed us of this episode. Our news programme has already broadcast a report on the wave of burglaries that have beset our town, and which Inspector Salvo Montalbano, into whose hands the case has unfortunately fallen, has been unable to put an end to. The thieves apparently always use the same modus operandi.

'They break into a holiday home while the owners are asleep inside, take the keys to their apartment in town, and then proceed to burgle it unmolested. This is exactly what happened again in the latest robbery, suffered by Miss Angelica Cosulich, but in his report on the incident,

Inspector Montalbano altered the facts, writing that the only place that was burgled was Miss Cosulich's apartment in town. Whereas the procedure was in fact the same on this occasion: the burglars first broke into the villa belonging to Miss Cosulich's cousin, while she was asleep inside, and took the keys to her urban apartment.

'This raises two questions. Was it Miss Cosulich who failed to tell Inspector Montalbano of the true sequence of events? And, if so, for what purpose? Or was it the inspector himself who filed a partial report of these events? And, if so, why? We shall keep our viewers informed of the latest developments in this situation, which we find gravely disturbing.'

'You wanted a reaction?' said Zito. 'Well, there you have it!'

*

Now Montalbano understood what had made Mr C'mishner so angry.

It was four-thirty, so he made his way slowly to Montelusa Central Police.

The usher showed him into the commissioner's office at five-twenty.

Montalbano felt calm. He'd had all the time he needed to prepare a dramatic defence, to be delivered in the old-fashioned Italian style of Gustavo Salvini or Ermete Zacconi.

The commissioner did not look up from a piece of paper he was reading. He did not greet the inspector or even tell him to sit down.

Notice to mariners: incoming high-intensity storm.

Then, still without saying a word, the commissioner extended his arm and handed Montalbano the paper he'd been reading.

It was an anonymous letter, written in block capitals.

IT ISN'T TRUE THAT THE BURGLARS ONLY BROKE INTO THE APARTMENT WHERE ANGELICA COSULICH LIVES. THEY TOOK THE KEYS FROM HER COUSIN'S VILLA, WHERE SHE HAD GONE TO TAKE THE DAY OFF. WHY DID INSPECTOR MONTALBANO OMIT THIS FACT FROM HIS REPORT?

Montalbano threw the paper disdainfully back on the commissioner's desk.

'I demand an explanation!' Bonetti-Alderighi said.

Montalbano brought his hand to his forehead, as if in pain.

'Alas!' he said operatically. 'What grave offence is this?'

Removing his hand from his brow, he opened his eyes wide, then pointed at the commissioner with a trembling finger.

'You insult me with such ignoble insults!'

'Come now, Montalbano, nobody is insulting you!' said the commissioner, slightly bewildered.

'You lend credence to the words of an anonymous

coward! You – yes, you – who should protect your faithful attendants, you abandon me to the whims of vile false-hoods!'

'Why are you talking that way? Come on, calm down!'

Montalbano didn't sit down so much as collapse into a chair.

'My report is honest and veracious! And none shall cast doubt upon it!'

'But why are you talking that way?' the commissioner repeated, seeming troubled.

'Could I have some water?'

'Help yourself.'

Montalbano stood up, took two steps, staggering as though drunk, opened the minibar, poured himself a glass of water, and sat back down.

'Now I feel a little better. Forgive me, Mr Commissioner, but when I am unjustly accused of something, I temporarily lose control of my language skills. It's called Scotti Turow syndrome; do you know it?'

'Vaguely,' said the commissioner, not wanting to appear completely ignorant. 'Now tell me what really happened.'

'Mr Commissioner, that letter is a pack of lies. While it's true that Miss Cosulich was sleeping in her cousin's villa—'

'But then—'

'Please let me finish. The burglars did not go inside the villa; they did not burgle it.'

Which was the pure and simple truth.

'But then how did they get their hands on the keys? Because you, in your report, write that the door to her apartment was not forced!'

'Let me explain. Miss Cosulich carelessly left the keys to her apartment in the glove compartment of her car, which was parked outside the villa. The thieves, apparently in passing, examined the documents with her address on it and decided to take advantage of the opportunity. Technically, I couldn't mention a burglary in the villa in the report, since this never happened. I wrote instead that the woman's car had been stolen. So, as you can see, there was no omission.'

He glanced at his watch. *Matre santa*, it was three minutes to six!

'I'm sorry, Mr Commissioner, but the *Butterfly* is about to come into port, and I—'

'Didn't you say it was called the *Pinkerton*?'

'Excuse me, you're absolutely right. The *Pinkerton*. You see, that unjust accusation has confused—'

'All right, all right, you can go.'

*

He raced to Marinella at breakneck speed, or about 80 kph for normal drivers.

As he was passing through the village of Villaseta, a carabiniere with signal discs in hand, who'd probably been hiding behind a blade of grass, suddenly appeared in front of him, gesturing for him to stop.

'Licence and registration.'

'Why, may I ask?'

'The speed limit in a residential area is fifty. Everybody and their dog knows this.'

The inspector's irritation at this new delay and the use of a cliché triggered an unfortunate reply.

'Why, don't the cats and birds know it?'

The carabiniere gave him a dirty look. 'Trying to be funny, are we?'

He couldn't allow himself to get into an argument. The man was likely to run him in, and that would be all for Angelica that night.

'I'm sorry.'

How humiliating, shameful, offensive for a police inspector to have to say he was sorry to an officer of the carabinieri!

The carabiniere, who was carefully studying the inspector's licence, made a strange face.

'Are you Inspector Montalbano?'

'Yes,' he admitted through clenched teeth.

'Are you on duty?'

Of course he was on duty. He was always on duty. 'Yes.'

'Then you can go,' said the officer, giving him back his licence and registration, and a military salute.

Montalbano drove off at a speed that would have had him finishing last in a tortoise race, but after the first bend he sped up to eighty again.

*

By the time he got home, it was six-forty.

It was anybody's guess now whether Angelica had phoned or not.

He took the phone off the hook so that it would be engaged, went and had a quick shower because he was drenched in sweat, then put the receiver back on the hook and got dressed.

His dramatic performance with the commissioner had taken a lot out of him.

At seven-thirty, after he had already smoked a whole pack of cigarettes, the phone decided to ring.

It was Angelica. 'There's a problem.'

What was going on? Was this National Frustration Day or something? 'What is it?'

'I'm at my cousin's villa. I came to put my room in order again. I hadn't been back since the burglary, you know, and suddenly the power went out. A fuse must have blown. I have everything I need here to fix it, but I don't know how to do it.'

'Sorry to ask, but what do you need power for right now? Just lock up, come over to my place, and tomorrow we'll call an electrician.'

'They're delivering the water tonight.'

'I don't understand.'

'They deliver water here once a week. If there's no electricity in the tank, the pump doesn't work, and the water won't be sucked in. Understand? I risk being without water for over a week.'

Montalbano had an unpleasant thought: Did she perhaps need her love nest in the coming days?

As if she'd read his mind, she said: 'And I won't be able to wash the floors, which are dirty.'

'I can try to fix things myself.'

'I didn't dare ask. I'll explain to you how to get here.'

✳

She'd certainly picked a nice place!

It was in the open country, and the inspector took forty-five minutes to get there.

Leading off an unmade road was a long lane with an iron gate that looked as if it hadn't been closed for years. At the end of it was a large eighteenth-century villa, completely isolated and well maintained.

He parked the car behind the villa.

Angelica was waiting for him at the top of the staircase that led to her room.

'Here I am!'

She smiled at him. And it was as if the sun, which was setting, had changed its mind and risen back into the sky.

Montalbano started climbing, and she came a few steps down. They embraced and kissed halfway. The inspector then said: 'Let's get going while there's still some light.'

She turned around, went back up the stairs, and disappeared into her room.

Montalbano began to climb but failed to see a stair and fell, causing a terrible pain in his ankle. He was barely able to suppress a string of curses.

Angelica rushed to his aid. 'Did you hurt yourself?'

'A little, in my . . . ankle.'

'Think you can walk?'

'Yes, let's not waste any time. It's going to get dark very soon.'

It didn't take him long to find the little box that brought the current from the villa to her room. He picked up a chair, climbed onto it, and removed the cover of the box.

A wire had short-circuited.

'Go down into the villa and turn off the power.' She opened a door and disappeared.

Montalbano took advantage of the situation to get a good look at the room.

It was rather spartan and must have been used for one purpose only. That one. And the observation put him in a dark, terrible mood.

Angelica returned. 'Done.'

'Get me some electrical tape.'

It took him barely two minutes to fix the problem. 'Go and turn the power back on.'

He remained standing on the chair, awaiting the result.

All at once the light in the middle of the room came on. '*Bravissimo!*' said Angelica, coming back into the room. 'Why don't you come down?' she added.

'You'll have to help me.'

She drew near, and, bracing himself with both hands on her shoulders, he carefully descended.

His ankle hurt like hell.

'Lie down on the bed,' said Angelica. 'I want to see what you're made of.'

He obeyed. She lightly pulled up his left trouser leg. 'Oh my God! It's so swollen!'

She took his shoe off with some difficulty, and then the sock, too.

'That's quite a sprain!'

She went into the bathroom and returned with a small tube in her hand.

'If nothing else, this will lessen the pain a little.'

She massaged him all around the ankle with the ointment.

'In about ten minutes, I'll put your sock back on.' And she came and lay down beside him.

Then she put her arms around him and rested her head on his chest.

Through Montalbano's head flashed the words:

That in this very bed on which he lies
His love has lain, and often, in the close
Embrace that nothing of herself denies.

And who knew with how many!

Flesh for hire. Males who took money to give pleasure.

How many pairs of eyes had seen her naked body? How many hands had caressed her on that bed?

And how many times had that room, which looked like a cell, heard her voice say, 'More . . . more . . .'

A fierce jealousy took hold of him. The worst kind, jealousy of the past.

But he could do nothing about it. He started trembling in anger, in fury.

No less abhorrence now our hero shows
And no less quickly from that bed he flies . . .

'I'm leaving!' he said, sitting up.

Angelica, confused, raised her head. 'What's got into you?'

'I'm leaving!' he repeated, putting his sock back on, and then his shoe.

Angelica must have intuited a little of what was going on in his mind, because she just lay there watching him, without saying another word.

Montalbano descended the staircase with teeth clenched

so he wouldn't cry out in pain, then got in his car, turned the key in the ignition, and drove off.

He was furious.

*

The moment he got home, he unplugged the phone and went and lay down in bed.

Four whiskies later, lying there with the bottle within reach, he felt his rage come down a few degrees.

And he began to think.

First of all, he had to take care of his ankle, otherwise he might not make it to work tomorrow.

He looked at the clock. Nine-thirty.

He called Fazio on his mobile and explained the situation. Saying, however, that he'd twisted his ankle stepping up from the beach to the veranda.

'I'll be there in half an hour with Licalzi,' said Fazio.

'Who's that?'

'He's the masseur of the Vigàta football team.'

He didn't even know Vigàta had a football team.

Despite the pain he was feeling and his displeasure over missing dinner with Angelica, he was hungry.

He got up, leaning on chairs and other pieces of furniture as he made his way to the kitchen.

In the fridge was a large platter of seafood salad. He ate it at the kitchen table, which he didn't bother to lay.

The moment he finished it, the doorbell rang. He went and answered the door.

'This is Mr Licalzi,' said Fazio.

Licalzi was a giant of about six foot three, with hands that were frightening just to look at. He was carrying a small black bag like the ones doctors use.

Montalbano lay back down in bed, and the man started fiddling with his foot and leg.

'It's nothing serious,' Licalzi said.

And when, in his life, had anything ever been serious? he thought bitterly to himself.

Or if, perchance, there had been something, the ridiculousness of the past twenty-four hours had completely effaced it.

Licalzi finished wrapping his foot nice and tight.

'It would probably be better if you didn't go out tomorrow morning but stayed at home and rested.'

Spending a whole morning alone with his thoughts, at this point in time, was really not an option for him.

'Impossible! I have a lot of work to do at the office!'

Fazio looked at him but said nothing.

'But driving is not—'

'I'll come at nine to pick him up,' said Fazio.

'A cane would be a good idea.'

'I'll bring him one myself,' Fazio intervened again.

'Well, be sure to get out of bed as little as possible, only for the strictest necessities,' Licalzi added.

Montalbano's eyes sought out Fazio's, who gestured 'no' with his head. He mustn't offer to pay the masseur.

'Thank you so very much,' Montalbano said, holding out his hand.

Then he made as if to get up, to see them out.

'Don't get up, we know the way,' Licalzi ordered him.

'G'night, Chief.'

'Thank you too, Fazio.'

'Don't mention it, Chief.'

*

Now came the hard part.

Despite what Licalzi had just told him, he got up, took the bottle, glass, cigarettes, and lighter, and went and sat down on the veranda.

The first fundamental point, essential to the reflection to come:

You, dear Salvo, are a first-class idiot, while Angelica is a genuine, upright person.

Had she ever hidden the existence of her love nest from him?

Or the reason she had one?

Wasn't it one of the first things she mentioned to him outright?

And what would he, on the other hand, have preferred?

For her to be a young virgin so like a rose, to say it again with Ariosto?

And for him to be the first to pluck that rose, *which no despoiling hand had ever touched?*

TEN

Had he gone completely dotty?

Or was this one of the first signs of the stupidity that comes with old age?

In her room he'd been overcome not by a fit of jealous rage, as he'd thought, but by a fit of senile imbecility.

And Angelica must have felt deeply offended and embittered by his behaviour.

She'd always played above board with him, and this was how he returned the favour?

During the night she spent in the car with him, as they were kissing, hugging, caressing one another, not once did she say, 'I love you,' or anything similar.

She'd been honest even then.

And he'd treated her the way he'd treated her.

Even Mr Z, in writing the anonymous letter to Ragonese . . .

Wait a second!

Stop right there, Montalbà!

When Bonetti-Alderighi made him read the letter, he'd noticed something strange that at the time hadn't quite rung true, but he'd been too wrapped up in the role he was playing to try to work out what it was.

What had that note said? Suddenly it all came back to him.

Mr Z, who accused him of omission, had on his own part omitted two important things, surely on purpose.

The first was that he mentioned only Angelica's cousin's villa and didn't say a word about her special room in that villa.

The second was that he'd entirely passed over Angelica's special use of that room.

In fact he'd written that Angelica had gone there to spend her day off, or something similar.

Whereas the burglars, when they went in, could see for themselves that the girl was sleeping with a man!

And so why had he omitted these two rather important details?

Did he want to make trouble for Montalbano while keeping Angelica's reputation intact? Why would he want to do that?

What sort of relationship could Mr Z have with Angelica?

This was something only she could explain. But this meant having to see her again.

And he had no intention of doing this.

Because the ridiculous scene in the love nest did at least have one positive result: it made him realize that his affair with Angelica could not continue.

Absolutely not.

It had been not so much an infatuation as a bout of madness.

He felt a lump in his throat.

He dissolved it with his tenth glass of whisky.

Then, resting his arms on the table, and his head on his arms, he fell asleep almost immediately, entirely numb from alcohol and self-pity.

Around five o'clock in the morning he dragged himself into bed.

*

'Wan' some caffee, Isspector?'

'Thanks, Adelì.'

He opened one eye, and about five minutes later managed to open the other one too. He had a mild headache.

The first cup of coffee revived him. 'Bring me another cup.'

The second one polished him up. The telephone rang.

He'd thought it was still unplugged. Maybe the housekeeper had plugged it back in.

'Adelì, you answer that. And tell them I can't get out of bed.'

He heard her talking but couldn't tell who with. Then Adelina came back to his room.

'A' wazza you girlfrenn. She gonna call you onna mobile phone.'

And so the little march began to sound.

'Where on earth were you last night? You have no idea how many times I tried to call!'

'I was out on a stakeout.'

'You could have told me!'

'I'm sorry, but I went directly there from the office. I didn't go home in between.'

'And why can't you get out of bed?'

'I twisted my ankle. It was night, you know, total darkness . . .'

Bravo, Montalbano! Tireless seeker of truth in public, incorrigible liar in private.

*

Fazio arrived at nine.

'Absolute calm at the Sciortinos' house.'

'Let's see what happens tonight.'

When it came time to put on his shoes, there was no way the left one would fit.

'Wear a shoe on your right foot and a slipper on your left,' Fazio suggested after having tried in vain to help him.

'I'll feel ridiculous coming to the office with one slipper.'

'Then just stay here; it's not like there's a whole lot to do. I'll come back in the afternoon with Licalzi.'

'Wait a second. Sit down. I have something to tell you. Yesterday, when the commissioner called me . . .'

He told him about the anonymous letter and what it said.

'Doesn't that seem strange to you?'

'It certainly does.'

'Don't you think it might not be a bad idea to question Miss Cosulich about it?'

'I think she's the only person who could give us an explanation,' said Fazio.

'Then call her and question her.'

Fazio gave him a bewildered look.

'The whole thing seems rather delicate to me. Why don't you do it yourself, tomorrow, since you seem to be on such familiar terms with her?'

'First of all, because we're losing time. And, anyway, what gives you the idea that I'm on more familiar terms with her than you are?'

Fazio didn't dare open his mouth.

'Call her this morning, even,' the inspector went on, 'and have her come in when she gets off work at the bank, which will be around six. Then come back here and report to me.'

*

He stayed in bed the rest of the morning, reading a novel.

He felt like a convalescent, not because of his foot but because of his heart.

At one o'clock, Adelina brought him lunch in bed.

Pasta *'ncasciata* (a sheer delight that can change the outlook even of someone on the verge of suicide). Squid cut up into rings and fried to a crisp. Fruit.

When Adelina finally went home, after leaving him his dinner for the evening, he became convinced that he would never digest properly while lying down.

So he got dressed, put on one shoe and one slipper — the beach, after all, was deserted — found the cane that Fazio had brought him, and took a long walk along the water's edge.

✳

Fazio came at around seven-thirty. 'Licalzi should be here any minute.'

Montalbano didn't give a flying fuck about Licalzi. He was interested in something else.

'Did you talk to La Cosulich?'

'Yes, sir. She was rather worried about you.'

Was he wrong, or was there a faint shadow of a smile playing on Fazio's lips?

Or did he think this merely because he had something to hide and everything seemed to be conspiring against him?

'Why was she worried?'

'Because her branch manager called her and told her what Ragonese had said on TV. He wanted an explanation. She hadn't heard anything about it before then. She pretended to be very surprised and confirmed that it was her place in Vigàta that had been robbed. But she was very worried about the possible consequences for you.'

Montalbano preferred not dwelling any further on the subject, as they were wandering onto dangerous terrain.

'Did you mention the part of the anonymous letter that didn't make sense to us?'

'Uh-huh.'

'And what did she say?'

'She said she couldn't explain it. Actually, she blushed and even mentioned that the burglars had in fact seen her sleeping with someone . . .'

This wasn't a very pleasurable subject either. 'And in conclusion?'

'In conclusion, she was left wondering, just like us.'

Did they enjoy following leads that went nowhere?

The doorbell rang. It was Licalzi.

'Did you stay in bed all day?'

'Of course!'

'In fact you seem almost healed.'

Apparently the long walk along the beach had done him good.

'Now I'm going to give you a massage, rub a bit of

cream on you, put the bandage back on, and, you'll see, tomorrow you'll be able to go back to work without any problem.'

He said it in a cheery tone, as if going back to work was even better than going dancing.

Licalzi's massaging of his ankle and the surrounding area made him think again of Angelica doing the same thing as he lay on her bed.

And at that moment a bright light rather like a camera flash lit up his brain.

When Licalzi had finished, Montalbano thanked him again, and since Fazio was making as if to leave, he stopped him.

'You stay behind another five minutes, please, Fazio.'

Fazio showed Licalzi out and then came back.

'What is it, Chief?'

'You have to talk with La Cosulich again, immediately.'

Fazio grimaced. 'Why?'

'Show her the list the Peritores drew up and ask her whether any of the men on the list have ever pursued her insistently, and whether she turned them down.'

Fazio made a doubtful face.

'It's an idea that came to me just now,' Montalbano continued. 'Suppose someone from the list was rejected by her; he could now have her in the palm of his hand and blackmail her. "If you don't sleep with me, I'll broadcast far and wide what you really do in your cousin's villa."'

'Sorry to say, Chief, but you seem fixated on the idea that Mr Z is someone on the list.'

'But why do you want to exclude him *a priori*? It's an avenue we have to explore. What have we got to lose?'

'All right, but why don't you explore this avenue yourself? You, with the ladies, you know what to do, whereas I . . .'

Montalbano decided to cut things short.

'No, you do it. Thanks for everything and good night. Oh, and if there's any news from the Sciortinos, give me a ring.'

✣

He'd just finished laying the table on the veranda, so he could enjoy the rice salad Adelina had made for him, when the telephone rang.

He didn't feel like talking to anyone, but then it occurred to him that it might be Livia calling to find out how his ankle was doing, and so he went to pick it up.

When he reached for the receiver, the phone fell silent.

If it was Livia, she would call back, since she knew he was immobilized at home.

He went back out to the veranda, sat down, and was bringing the first forkful to his lips when the phone started ringing again.

He got up, cursing the saints. 'Hello!'

'Please don't hang up.' It was Angelica.

His heart began to race, of course, but not as fast as he would have thought.

A sign that he was getting better. 'I won't hang up. What is it?'

'Three things, really quick. First, I wanted to know how your foot is doing.'

'A lot better, thanks. Tomorrow I can go back to work.'

'Have you had a lot of trouble over . . . that favour you did for me?'

'I was called in by the commissioner after Ragonese sent him the anonymous letter he'd received, but I managed to convince him that I'd told the truth in my report. I don't think there'll be any unpleasant consequences for me.'

'But there will be for me.'

'How?'

'The manager of my branch felt obliged to write to the head office.'

'Why?'

'Because he says he's very troubled by the conjecture that newsman made – that is, that I may have lied. He says it's bad publicity for the bank and that, however things turn out, my credibility as an employee has been diminished.'

She certainly had a lovely voice . . . It was spellbinding, like the song of the sirens. It soothed you, it . . .

He managed to shake off the spell.

'What does that mean in plain language?'

'That I might be transferred.'

'I'm sorry.'

He meant it.

'So am I. One last thing, and then I'll let you go. Fazio asked me whether anyone on the Peritores' list had pursued me insistently and was rejected. The answer is yes, a lot of the men on that list have pursued me, to the point of harassment at times, but I don't think any of them would be capable of blackmail.'

'It was just a hypothesis of mine.'

'Well, I have one of my own.'

'And what's that?'

'Clearly whoever wrote that anonymous letter knows my . . . well, my habits. But he didn't reveal them. That would have ruined me. So why did he do it? Now let's assume that this is a person I know, say, a bank customer, who is trying to win my sympathies . . .'

'I don't understand. Do you mean in order to get a loan?'

Angelica started laughing. My God, what a laugh!

Montalbano's heart, which until that moment had been pumping like a steam engine, suddenly turned into an electric high-speed train.

'With me as the loan,' Angelica said when she finished laughing.

That didn't sound like such a bad idea.

But it was too generic. He needed Angelica to say more, perhaps to give a few names of those who had pressed the issue a little more than the others.

'What were you doing?' Angelica asked.

'Eating dinner.'

'I haven't eaten.'

Then, just to keep talking, he asked: 'Where are you?'

'Here.'

'Where's here?'

'Here, in Marinella.'

He started. Why was she in Marinella? 'What are you doing here?'

'Waiting for you to open the door for me.'

He thought he perhaps hadn't heard right. 'What did you say?'

'I said I'm waiting for you to open the door for me.'

He staggered and grabbed a chair for support, as if he'd just been clubbed in the head.

He set the phone down on the table, went to the door, and looked through the peephole.

There was Angelica, holding her mobile phone to her ear. Ever so slowly, Montalbano opened the door.

And he knew, as he was doing it, that he was opening not only the front door to his house, but the door to his personal damnation, his own private hell.

*

'Care to join me for dinner?'

'Yes. I've finally managed to make it happen.'

He sat her down beside him, so she could look at the sea.

'It's so beautiful here!'

He shared his seafood salad with her.

And they didn't say another word until they had finished eating.

But Montalbano was curious about something.

'I'm sorry, but . . . why didn't it occur to you that I might not be able . . . ?'

'To open the door for me?'

'Yes.'

'Because there might have been someone else with you inside?'

'Yes.'

'But didn't your girlfriend leave a few days ago?'

Montalbano's mouth opened of its own accord. Then he closed it and started to speak again, but he stammered more than spoke.

'But . . . what . . . how . . . do you know . . . what . . .'

'I know everything about you. Your age, your habits, what you think about certain things . . . As soon as you left my place that day after the burglary, I quickly got on the phone and found out what I needed to know.'

'And so when I invited you to eat at Enzo's, you already knew that I always eat there?'

'Of course. And I also knew that you don't like to talk while you're eating.'

'And you pretended to—'

'Yes, I pretended.'

'But why?'

'Because I liked you from the start,' said Angelica.

Better change the subject.

'Listen, I'd like to take advantage of this opportunity . . .'

She smiled slyly.

'No, not in your bed.'

'Can't you be serious for a moment?'

'It's hard for me to be serious when I'm happy. But I'll try.'

'A few minutes ago you said the writer of the anonymous letter may have been trying to win your sympathies.'

'Why, don't you agree?'

'It's possible, because, you see, I'd been thinking the same thing. But couldn't you give me some names?'

'Of whom?'

'Of men outside the Peritores' circle who may have pushed a little too hard with you . . .'

She shrugged.

'There's an embarrassment of riches.'

'I'm asking you to overcome your embarrassment and make a few choices.'

'Well, that's a big responsibility.'

'Oh, come on!'

'It is! I give you a name without a second thought, and the poor man will suddenly find himself up to his neck in—'

'I'm not asking you to give me a name without a second thought.'

She said nothing, and just stared out at the sea.

ELEVEN

'Have you got any whisky?' she asked out of the blue.

'Of course.'

Montalbano got up, went to get the bottle and two glasses, returned to the veranda, and poured out two fingers' worth for her and four for himself.

'Come on now, a level playing field,' Angelica protested.

Montalbano added two more fingers to her glass. 'Would you like some ice with that?'

'No, I like it neat. Like you.'

They drank their first sips.

'It's not easy. I have to think it over carefully.'

'OK.'

'Tell you what. Come to my place tomorrow for dinner, and I'll give you the names.'

'All right.'

She finished drinking her whisky and stood up.

'I'm going to go. And thanks. For everything.'

Montalbano saw her to the door.

Just before going out, Angelica put her lips on his for a brief moment.

Sitting on the veranda again, Montalbano didn't know whether to feel disappointed or pleased with the encounter.

From the moment he'd opened the door for her, he'd been simultaneously hoping and dreading.

And so, he concluded, it couldn't possibly have gone any better than it did.

✳

Around three-thirty in the morning he thought he heard the telephone ringing.

He got up in a daze, crashed into a chair, but managed in the dark to pick up the receiver.

'Hello?'

'It's Fazio, Chief.'

'What's going on?'

'There's been an exchange of fire with the burglars at the Sciortinos'. Shall I come and get you? I have to drive past your place anyway.'

'All right.'

✳

In ten minutes he was ready. His foot fitted perfectly into the shoe, and he wasn't even limping.

Fazio arrived five minutes later. They drove off towards Punta Bianca.

'Anybody wounded?'

'They shot at Loschiavo but didn't get him. That's all I know.'

*

The Sciortinos' cottage was brightly lit up. Mrs Sciortino was making coffee for everyone.

The couple from Rome, whose name was De Rossi, were rather upset, and for them Mrs Sciortino made some camomile tea.

Montalbano and Fazio called Loschiavo aside and walked down to the sea with him.

'Tell us what happened,' said Montalbano.

'I was in a squad car on the hill at the back, Inspector, when suddenly I saw a car come up the beach with its headlights off. I looked at my watch, and it was five minutes to three. I got out of the car and started making my way down the hill without being noticed. It was very dark, and I fell twice. Then I hid behind a large rock.'

'How many were there?'

'Three men. I think they were wearing ski masks, but it was very dark, as I said. Then after a while I didn't see them any more. The house was between me and them and prevented me from seeing what they were doing. So I started moving and made my way behind the house. I stuck my head around the corner and watched. They were busy doing something outside the front door. So I pulled out my weapon and said, "Stop, police!" I saw a flash and heard a crack. I returned fire and shot three times, taking cover. But they kept firing non-stop, preventing me from sticking my head back out. Then I heard their car drive away at high speed.'

'Thanks; you've been very precise.' Then, to Fazio: 'But where have the Sciortinos and everyone else gone off to?'

'I'll go and see,' said Fazio. 'Did you want to question them?'

'No, but I don't understand why they all suddenly went back into the house, all at the same time.'

'You did a good job,' Montalbano said to Loschiavo as Fazio was walking away. 'Do you think any of your shots hit anyone?'

'I went and looked immediately afterwards, but I didn't see any traces of blood on the ground.'

Fazio came back.

'They've decided to go back to Vigàta. He said they were afraid to stay here.'

'But the thieves definitely won't be back,' said the inspector. 'You know what I say? I say we go home and get a few hours of sleep. You can go too, Loschiavo.'

✳

'Ah, Chief, Chief! Wha', d' jou hoitcha foot? Ya gonna hafta walk witta cane f'r ivver?' Catarella asked with concern.

'No, come on! I'm fine! I just brought the cane to give it back to Fazio.'

'Jeez, I'm rilly glad, Chief.'

'Is Fazio here?'

'He called sayin' 'e'd be 'ere in about ten minnits.'

Montalbano went into his office.

He'd been away for only a day, but it felt more like a month.

On his desk, aside from some fifty documents to sign, were six personal letters addressed to him.

His right hand shot out and grabbed one.

The same envelope as last time, same handwriting, except that this time the letter hadn't been posted but hand delivered.

He picked up the receiver.

'Catarella, come in here for a second.'

'Yessir, Chief.'

How did he always manage to get there so fast? Did he dematerialize in his telephone cupboard and rematerialize inside the inspector's office?

'Who brought this letter?'

'A li'l boy, Chief. Five minnits afore ya got 'ere.'

A classic arrangement.

'Did he say anything?'

''E said the litter was sint by summon you know.'
Right. Indeed he knew exactly who'd sent it.
Mr Z.
'Thanks, you can go.'
He decided to open the envelope.

Dear Montalbano,

You've shown yourself to be quite intelligent, which I never doubted.

But you were also aided by luck or some other factor that I have yet to identify.

At any rate this letter is to confirm that there will be a fourth and last burglary. By the end of the week.

And it will be a total success.

If you haven't already come to this conclusion you should know that last night's burglary had a purpose.

Which was to find out whether you had worked things out.

And since you prepared a good defence, I shall now be forced to change tactics.

At any rate, score one point in your favour.

Cordially yours.

'What do you think?'
Fazio put the letter down on the desk. He had a slight look of disgust on his face.
'I think Mr Z is claiming that he organized the

burglary just to see whether or not you understood his moves. He is very pretentious; you were right.'

'But it's the second sentence I can't quite work out,' said Montalbano. 'What do you think he means when he says we were aided by a factor he hasn't managed to identify yet?'

'No idea.'

'And there are some other things that don't make sense to me.'

'In the letter?'

'No, in Mr Z's behaviour.'

'And what would they be?'

'It's not clear to me, but maybe it'll become clear as we talk about it.'

'So talk, then.'

'It concerns last night's attempted burglary of the Sciortino house. Lojacono, Peritore, Cosulich, and Sciortino are all friends, all part of the same broader circle of acquaintances, and all on the famous list. This you cannot deny.'

'And indeed I don't. I only want to remind you that the Sciortinos didn't tell any of their friends that they were going to Punta Bianca for a few days.'

'Now I've got you! And what if Sciortino or his wife happened to mention my phone call to some friends? The one where I asked them if they'd told anyone they were going to Punta Bianca?'

'I don't get the—'

'Let me finish. The instant Mr Z finds out about our phone call, he organizes the theft!'

'But what is he, some kind of idiot? He should have understood from our phone call that the house was under surveillance!'

'Exactly!'

'Chief, if you don't make yourself clearer . . .'

'It's a perfect opportunity for him! It's a way for him to show that he's not part of the Peritores' circle of friends. He pretends not to know that the house is under surveillance! It's another red herring, can't you see? Because, if I fall for it, I should start looking for the ring-leader outside that damned list!'

'Chief, when you get something into your head . . . Whatever way I look at it, I still maintain that Mr Z is one of the people on the list! You know what I'm going to do? I'm going to call Sciortino and ask him if he told any of his friends about our phone call.'

'You'll be making a mistake! Instead you should let him think he managed to fool us!'

'Whatever you say.' Then Fazio added: 'Something just occurred to me.'

'Let's hear it.'

'At the moment I have seven men and two cars at my disposal. Going by the names on the list, there are still fourteen apartments left to be burgled. But they're all relatively close to one another. I might just be able to put all of them under surveillance until Saturday night.'

'With two cars?'

'Two cars and five bicycles, like the night watchmen.'

'All right, then, go ahead and try.'

Montalbano paused. Now he had to broach an uncomfortable subject.

'There's something else I have to tell you.'

'I'm listening.'

'Last night La Cosulich called me.'

He disliked lying to Fazio, but he didn't feel like telling him the truth, either.

'What did she want?'

'She said she had second thoughts about what she'd said to you. And she wondered whether Mr Z didn't reveal that she uses the villa as a love nest because he wants to blackmail her in the future.'

Fazio thought about this for a minute.

'It's a hypothesis worth considering. However, if you accept it, you end up in a contradiction.'

'I know what you're getting at. Since La Cosulich has excluded the men named on the list, Mr Z can't be part of the Peritores' circle of friends. But, given the point we're at now, I don't think we can leave a single stone unturned.'

'I agree with you, as far as that goes. Does Cosulich suspect anyone in particular?'

'She said she'll give me some names this evening. She invited me for dinner at her place.'

Fazio had an expression like a light bulb burning out. 'What's wrong?'

'What's wrong is that it's imprudent, Chief. Sorry to say.'

'But why?'

'Chief, that idiot journalist has already insinuated on TV that you might be covering for the girl. Just imagine what would happen if somebody saw you go to Cosulich's house in the evening!'

'You're right. I hadn't thought of that.'

'And you can't very well take her out to a restaurant again, either.'

'So what should I do, then?'

'Have her come here to the station.'

'And what if she doesn't want to?'

'If she doesn't want to, then it's better for her to come to your house in Marinella, late in the evening, when it'll be harder for them to see her.'

But were Fazio's eyes smiling? Was the little bastard having fun?

'I'll have her come here,' Montalbano said decisively.

'It's the best thing,' said Fazio, standing up.

*

The inspector was reaching for the phone to call Angelica when his hand froze in mid-air.

The call would be answered by the bank's telephone operator. And he would be forced to say he was Inspector Montalbano.

And couldn't a phone call from the police further compromise Angelica's already shaky standing at the bank?

So how was he going to get in touch with her? He had an idea.

He called Catarella.

'Yessir.'

'Cat, do you know if anyone here is a customer at the Banca Siculo-Americana?'

'Yessir, Chief. Afficer Arturo Ronsisvalle. I went wit' 'im once issomuch as 'e 'ad a cheque an'—'

'Tell him to come to my office.'

While waiting, he picked up a piece of paper and wrote:

Please call me at the office as soon as you can. Thanks, Montal-bano.

This way, if any of Angelica's colleagues saw it, there was nothing to find fault with. He put the sheet of paper in an unaddressed envelope.

'You asked for me, Inspector?'

'Yes, listen, Ronsisvalle, do you know Angelica Cosu-lich?'

'I do. I'm a customer at the Banca—'

'I know. I want you to go to the bank and give her this letter, but without anyone noticing.'

'I'll say I want a printout of my account balance as an excuse.'

'Good. Thanks.'

✻

Half an hour later, Angelica called. 'What's going on?'

'Can you talk?'

'Yes.'

'I thought it might be unwise for me to come to your place. Somebody might see me.'

'Who the hell cares?'

'Actually, you should care. Think about it. Among other things, the Peritores live on the same street as you. If anybody should find out, the rumour that you and I have an understanding will gain momentum and become harder and harder to deny.'

She sighed. A few moments later she said:

'I guess you're right. But what are we going to do?'

'You could come to the station.'

'No.'

An immediate, decisive reply. 'Why not?'

'For the same reason that you won't come to my place.'

'What's the connection? I might have called you in for a detailed account of the burglary.'

'No. I just know it would be a mistake, I can feel it.'

'You could come to my place.'

'I'm delighted to accept the invitation. But, I'm sorry,

isn't it the same if someone sees me going to your place?'

'First of all, my house is isolated, and there are no neighbours nearby. And if you come at ten p.m., I assure you you won't run into anybody.'

'At this point I have an alternative proposition,' said Angelica.

'And what's that?'

She told him.

But it was not the sort of thing he should mention to Fazio.

✻

He took the list and read it for the umpteenth time.

1) P.I. Leone Camera and wife.
What did P.I. stand for? Private investigator?

2) Dr Giovanni Sciortino and wife.
This was the couple at whose house the attempted burglary occurred.

3) Dr Gerlando Filippone and wife.
Find out more about.

4) Emilio Lojacono, Esq., and wife.
This was the lawyer who suffered the first burglary when he was with his lover, Ersilia Vaccaro.

5) Giancarlo de Martino, engineer.
The one convicted for aiding and abetting an armed gang.

6) *Matteo Schirò, accountant.*
Unmarried? Find out more about.

7) *Mariano Schiavo, accountant, and wife.*
Find out more about.

8) *Mario Tavella, accountant, and wife.*
This was the one swimming in gambling debt.

9) *Dr Antonino Pirrera and wife.*
Find out more about.

10) *Stefano Pintacuda, Esq., and wife.*
Owns a holiday home. Find out more about.

11) *Dr Ettore Schisa.*
Unmarried? Find out more about.

12) *Antonio Martorana and wife.*
The surveyor Martorana's wife is apparently de Martino's mistress. Find out more about.

13) *Giorgio Maniace, surveyor.*
Fazio said this man was a widower. Was that his only good quality? What did he do in life? He also had a holiday home. And what else? Find out more about.

14) *Miss Angelica Cosulich.*
This one he knew all too well.

15) Francesco Costa.
Must be the most ignorant of the lot, since he didn't have any titles or degrees. Find out more about.

16) Agata Cannavò.
The widow and gossip. The one who thought she knew everything about everyone. Find out more about.

17) Dr Ersilia Vaccaro (and husband).
She was the lover of the lawyer Lojacono, fine. But why was the mention of her husband in parentheses?

18) Gaspare Di Mare, Esq., and wife.
Find out more about.

In conclusion, whatever Fazio might think, they had taken this list a little too lightly. There were quite a few people on it they knew nothing about.

Almost certainly Angelica could tell him something about them.

He folded the list back up and put it in his jacket pocket.

TWELVE

It was time to go and eat.

He left his office and, when walking past Catarella, noticed that he was so engrossed in his computer that he didn't even realize the inspector was there.

'What are you doing?'

Catarella very nearly fell out of his chair, then shot to his feet, as red-faced as a turkeycock.

'Well, sintz there in't no phone traffic, I's jess passin' the time playin'.'

'On the computer?'

'Yessir, Chief.'

'What kind of game?'

'Iss a game whereats to play it, 'ere's gotta be two o' yiz.'

'But there aren't two of you.'

''Ass true, but the 'pewter don't know I'm alone.'

This was also true.

'Tell me what the game consists of.'

'Well, Chief, iss azackly the appazit o' the game o' "screw-your-friend".'

'Explain.'

'Well, the game cossitts o' doin' a most damage y' can do to the apposing couple, who'd be the avversary, bu' also tryin' a proteck y'r own partner from danger.'

'So how are things going?'

'Right nows I'm in rilly big danger, bu' my partner, who's me m'self, 's comin' a lenn me a hand.'

'Good luck.'

'Tanks, Chief.'

*

'Listen, Enzo.'

'What is it, Inspector?'

'This evening, around seven . . . that girl who ate with me the other day, remember her . . . ?'

'How could I forget?'

'. . . she's going to drop off a little package for me. I'll come and get it around eight.'

'All right. What shall I bring you now?'

'Everything.'

He wouldn't admit it to himself, but he was pleased.

*

Later, sitting on the flat rock, his mood changed.

He was like a crocodile that shed tears as an effect of digestion.

He bitterly acknowledged that he was moving slowly, dragging the investigation behind him.

He was doing everything according to logic.

What was missing was the sudden flash, the lightning-quick intuition that leapt over all logical connections and in other situations had led him straight to the solution.

Was it his age?

He felt as if his brain was rusty, like a car left too long unused.

Or was it the cumbersome, continuous presence of Angelica in his thoughts, preventing him from taking that leap forward?

He felt broken in two.

Half of Montalbano told him to make sure he never saw her again.

The other half could think of nothing but the next moment he would have her beside him.

'How am I going get out of this?' he asked a crab that was having a rougher time than him climbing the rock.

He received no reply.

✳

'Did you call Miss Cosulich?' Fazio asked when he came in.

'Yeah, she doesn't want to come to the station.'

'So what are you going to do?'

'She says she'll call me tonight at home.'

Matre santa, what a tangle of lies he was forced to move about in!

'Chief, I had an idea.'

'Let's hear it.'

'Since you'll be talking to La Cosulich this evening, why don't you ask her for some information about her friends? . . . You know, gossipy stuff.'

'About the friends on the Peritores' list?'

'That's right.'

'So you're coming around to my idea?'

'I'm just following your lead, leaving no stone unturned.'

'OK, have a look.'

He took the list out of his pocket and showed it to Fazio.

'I'd already thought of the same thing as you. There are four names that I'm particularly interested in.'

'Which ones?'

'Schirò, Schisa, Maniace, and Costa.'

'And why's that?'

'Because they're either unmarried or widowers.' Fazio looked bewildered.

'For somebody who gets it in his head to become the mastermind of a burglary ring,' the inspector explained, 'a wife represents a problem.'

'But she could be an accomplice.'

'Right. Nevertheless, if we can manage to find out a little more about these four, we will have taken a step forward.'

'If you want, I can do some research myself.'

'Of course I want you to!'

He was glad Fazio wasn't putting up any more resistance about the list.

*

Around eight o'clock he stopped at Enzo's to pick up his packet.

When he got home, he put the packet on the table and opened the refrigerator to see what Adelina had made for him.

Rice *sartù*, fritters of *nunnatu*, and a platter of baby prawns to be dressed with olive oil, lemon, and salt.

He laid the table on the veranda and started eating slowly, alternating mouthfuls with breaths of sea air.

When he finished, it was ten-thirty. He cleared the table and rang Livia.

'Hi. I'm calling because I'm about to go out and probably won't be back till late.'

'The usual stakeout?'

He didn't like the tone Livia used in asking that question.

'I'll be up all night and all you can do is be snide about it?'

'I'm sorry, I wasn't being snide; it was the last thing on my mind.'

So was it him, with his bad conscience, who was misinterpreting everything?

He felt like a worm. Not only did he tell Livia lies, but he even accused her of intentions she didn't have.

Inspector Montalbano wasn't liking himself at all.

When he got off the phone, he opened the packet.

Inside were two keys, one small and one large. He dropped them into his pocket, put on his jacket, and went out.

*

When he got to the posh part of town – which by the light of the crescent moon looked more like a nightmare from overeating than a residential area – he turned onto Via Costantino Nigra, a parallel street running behind Via Cavour's buildings.

As soon as he was behind the one shaped like an ice-cream cone, he stopped and parked.

But he waited five minutes before getting out.

Then, seeing that there wasn't a soul on the streets and all the windows in the nearby buildings were dark, he quickly got out of the car, locked it, crossed the street, and went up to the service entrance of Angelica's building.

He opened the door with three turns of the little key, went in, then locked the door behind him.

He found himself inside a large space lit with fluorescent lights and cluttered with bicycles and motor scooters.

On the left was a staircase leading to the upper floors, with a lift directly opposite. He opened the door, went in, and pressed the button for the top floor. It was slow, a typical freight lift.

On his way up to his earthly paradise, the usual snake that can be found in such surroundings hissed in his ear:

You're surely not the first to travel this secret path! It's anybody's guess how many have made the same journey!

But the snake did not succeed in its intent. All it did was point out things that he could imagine all by himself, knowing Angelica's habits.

The lift stopped. He had arrived. The door opened, he stepped out.

He was breathing heavily, panting, as if he had climbed the six storeys on foot.

Before ringing the doorbell, he decided he should try to calm down a little.

When his breathing returned to normal, he extended a finger to press the button.

And at that moment the other half of Montalbano said:

You're fucking up big-time!

Without knowing exactly how, he found himself back in the lift, ready to renounce paradise.

Then he heard Angelica's voice.

'What are you doing in the lift?'

He reopened the door. By now his fate was sealed.

'I dropped my lighter.'

She smiled at him.

And, dazzled by that smile, he let her take him by the hand and lead him inside.

The spaceship apartment was in perfect order and looked as if the burglars had never set foot in it.

'But what did they steal of yours?' he couldn't help but ask.

'Haven't you seen the list?'

'No.'

'Well, a tidy sum's worth of jewellery and furs.'

'Where did you keep them?'

'The jewellery? In a little safe in my study, hidden behind a painting. I spend all my money on jewellery, you know. I inherited quite a bit from my mother, too, and I guess I picked up her passion for it. The furs on the other hand were in the wardrobe.'

'But couldn't you have kept it all at your bank?'

'Yes, but it wouldn't have been a good idea. It would only have fed all the gossip about me. But did you come here to interrogate me?'

'No. I came to find out—'

'Come on, let's go out on the terrace.'

'What if somebody sees us?'

'They can't. Trust me.' He followed her.

The terrace was huge, as he'd imagined. But he was most impressed by the great quantity of plants, scents, and roses.

> Not far away she sees a charming nook
> Where flowering thorn with the vermilion red
> Of roses is made gay . . .

Oh, no! Not Ariosto again!

But there was nothing he could do about it. The Angelica he had beside him corresponded too closely with the one from his adolescent memories.

He felt as if he was in the Garden of Eden. The scent of jasmine dulled his senses.

Angelica turned on a little lamp that gave off a wan light.

'Where should we sit?'

There were only two possibilities.

A very low sort of beach bed, wide enough to fit two people, and a three-seater swing.

Both the little bed and the swing had a small table beside them, with whisky, glasses, and ashtray.

'Let's go on the swing,' Montalbano said prudently. It was comfortable and covered with cushions. And it was very close to the outside wall and therefore not visible from the buildings nearby.

'Whisky?'

'Yes.'

Angelica filled a glass halfway, handed it to him, and poured herself half a glass as well. Then she went and turned off the light.

'It'll only attract mosquitoes.' She sat down beside Montalbano.

'Do you tend the plants yourself?'

'I couldn't even if I wanted to. A gardener comes twice a week at six in the morning. He's a bit expensive, but I love my flowers, my roses, too much to do without them.'

Silence fell.

He was looking at Angelica's profile, which could have been drawn by a great master, and her long hair, which swayed imperceptibly in the air, lightly tossed every so often by a faint breeze as tender as a caress.

She was so beautiful!

His whole being wanted her, but part of his brain was still putting up resistance.

The swing's rocking motion brought their bodies into contact.

And neither of them made as if to move away.

On the contrary. Without seeming to, they each pressed harder against the other.

Montalbano enjoyed her warmth against the side of his body.

Then Angelica moved towards him, and he felt the sweet sensation of a breast resting against his arm. He wished they could stay like that all night.

And what a sky there was!

The stars looked as if they'd come much closer to earth, while a point of light, perhaps a weather balloon, was slowly navigating eastwards.

Matre santa, that scent of jasmine! It made his head spin!

And the movement of the swing, back and forth, rocked him gently, enchanting him, relaxing his muscles and nerves . . .

Throwing fuel on the fire, Angelica started softly humming a melody that sounded a lot like a lullaby . . .

He closed his eyes.

All at once he felt Angelica's lips on his, pressing hard, with passion.

He lacked the will to resist.

＊

He looked at the clock. It was half-past four. He got out of bed.

'You're leaving already?'

'It'll be dawn soon.'

He went into the bathroom to get dressed, feeling too embarrassed to let her see him.

When he was ready to go, Angelica, in her dressing gown, threw her arms around his neck and kissed him.

'Will I see you tomorrow?'

'Let's call each other.' She walked him to the lift and kissed him again.

✶

When he got home it was five o'clock. He sat down on the veranda.

He'd gone to Angelica's to find out the names of her most dogged pursuers, but had learned nothing.

No. He had to be honest with himself.

He'd gone there mostly in the secret hope that what happened would happen.

Nevertheless, he'd realized something important. Which was that the Angelica who had made love to him was a woman like any other, even if she was much more beautiful than the others.

What had he expected?

Something out of a chivalric romance?

Son et lumière?

Violins playing in the background, like at the movies? Whereas the whole thing had been almost banal, nothing out of the ordinary, almost a disappointment.

In the end, it had turned out to be a sort of exchange of bodies.

She wanted his, and he wanted hers.

They'd solved the problem, and a good night to all. Better friends than before.

Orlando, now a man again and wise
(Still manlier and wiser than before),
Discovered he was cured of love likewise.

The one whom he was wont so to adore,
Who was so fair and queenly in his eyes,
He now dismisses and esteems no more.

As he got undressed to go back to bed he realized he hadn't given Angelica her keys back.

He put them down on the table.

But he knew he would never use them again.

❊

He had hoped to sleep for three hours or so, but there was no way he could fall asleep.

Because the moment he closed his eyes, a sort of unease began to hound him, and he knew that the cause of it was what he'd done with Angelica.

Try as he might to repeat to himself that the woman was for ever gone from his heart, the undeniable fact was that she'd been in that heart, and how!

And facts have weight. They're not easily erased. They're not like words carried by the wind . . .

How could it have happened? He didn't even have the excuse of Livia being far away. Livia had been with him until the day before, but the minute she'd turned her back, he hadn't wasted a minute letting himself be swept away by the longing for another woman.

For so many years of his life there had been only Livia.

Then, after reaching a certain age, he was no longer able to remain indifferent to the many opportunities. A desire for youth? Fear of old age? He'd invoked them all; it was useless now to repeat the litany. Still, he felt they were insufficient explanations.

Maybe if he talked about it with someone . . . But who?

✶

Then, through the fog of the half-sleep into which he had drifted at around seven-thirty, he heard the phone ringing incessantly.

He got out of bed, walked towards the telephone with his eyes closed, and picked up the receiver.

'Hello?' he said in a voice from beyond the grave.

'Hi, it's Angelica. Did I wake you?'

He felt no emotion at the sound of her voice. 'No.'

'Come on, you're as hoarse as a—'

'I was just gargling.'

'Listen, did you by any chance tell Fazio that you'd be seeing me?'

'No, I said you'd be calling me on the phone.'

'Well, I'm feeling generous and want to spare you any embarrassment. Have you got paper and pen handy?'

'Yes.'

'Then write down the following. Michele Pennino, Via De Gasperi 38. Forty years old, unmarried. He's a customer at the bank, and extremely rich, but I don't know what he does for a living. He literally lost his head over me. When he finally realized that no really meant no, he closed his account and went and told the branch manager that it was because I had always treated him badly. Did you write that down?'

'Yes, go on.'

'The other man's name is Eugenio Parisi, Via del Gambero 21. He's married with two children, fifty years old. I met him at a party. You have no idea how many bouquets of roses, pastries, and even a necklace, which I returned to him . . . He got his revenge by sending an anonymous letter to my boyfriend, whose address he'd managed to find, I don't know how. The letter basically said I was a whore.'

'But how can you be so sure that he was the—?'

'From certain details that would take too long to explain.'

A thought came into the inspector's mind. 'Do you still have that letter?'

'No, are you kidding? Anyway, that's all I had to tell you. Listen, will you be coming this evening to . . . ?'

Montalbano closed his eyes and took the plunge.

'Ah, I wanted to tell you that you can drop by Enzo's this afternoon to pick up the little box with the keys.'

The minute he'd said it he regretted it. But he bucked up and bit his tongue.

She remained silent for a moment, then said:

'OK, I get it. *Ciao.*'

'*Ciao.*'

Putting down the receiver, he let out a cry exactly like Tarzan's in the jungle.

He'd liberated himself.

THIRTEEN

He hadn't made it back to the bedroom before the phone rang again.

'Hello?'

'Good morning.' It was Livia. 'I tried earlier, but the phone was busy. Who were you talking to?'

A courageous thought came into his head. Why not tell her everything?

Livia of course would feel resentful at first, but once her anger had subsided, she might even be able to help him . . .

She was the only person in the world who understood him even better than he understood himself.

He felt himself sweating all over.

'Well, what's come over you? Who were you talking to?'

He inhaled deeply.

'To a woman.' There, he'd done it.

'And what did she want?'

'Can you wait just a second?'

'Of course.'

He ran into the kitchen, drank a glass of water, dashed into the bathroom and washed his face, then went back to the phone.

'What did that woman want from you?'

Come on, Montalbano! Buck up, fire away!

'Well, we'd spent the night together . . .'

'In what sense?'

'What do you mean in what sense? We slept together.'

There was a pause.

'So when you told me you were going on a stakeout you were lying?'

'Yes.'

Another terrible pause.

Montalbano, standing stock-still, was waiting for the Great flood to begin. Instead he heard her laughing giddily. Was she so upset by his confession that she was losing her senses?

'Livia, please, don't do that! Don't laugh!'

'I'm not falling for it, darling!'

He felt befuddled, annihilated. She didn't believe him! 'I have no idea why you want to make me jealous, but I'm not buying it. As if you would ever tell me when you've been with another woman! You would sooner be flayed alive than admit it! Is this some kind of joke? Well, it hasn't worked.'

'Livia, listen to me, I—'

'You know what I say? I'm fed up!' She hung up.

Montalbano stood there in a daze, receiver in hand.

*

He went back to bed, utterly drained.

He lay there with his eyes shut, not thinking about anything.

About half an hour later he heard the front door open.

'Is that you, Adelì?'

'Yessah, iss me.'

'Make me a big mug of strong coffee, would you?'

*

When he got to the office it was almost ten o'clock. 'Send me Fazio,' he said to Catarella.

'Straightaways, Chief.'

Fazio came in carrying a stack of papers, which he laid on the desk.

'All to be signed. No news last night.'

'So much the better.'

Fazio sat down.

'Chief, yesterday you gave me four names we need to know more about.'

'Yeah, and so?'

'I only had time to ask around town about Maniace. I'll ask about the others today.'

'And what can you tell me about Maniace?'

'Can I take out the piece of paper I have in my pocket?'

'Only on condition that you don't give me any records-office information.'

Fazio suffered from what Montalbano called the 'records-office complex'. For every person he sought information about, Fazio would obtain heaps of useless details such as the father's name, the mother's maiden name, the place and time of birth down to the minute, prior places of residence, names and ages of any children, close relatives, distant relatives . . . A real obsession.

Fazio cast a glance at his scrap of paper, put it back into his pocket, and began.

'Giorgio Maniace is a land surveyor of forty-three and is, as I believe I already told you, a widower. He is president of the town's Catholic Men's Association.'

'That doesn't mean anything. Except for the foreigners from Third World countries, ninety-nine per cent of the criminals we send to jail in this country are Catholics and love the Pope.'

'Fine, but this seems to me a special case. Maniace comes from a rich family. And up until the age of thirty-five, he had an easy time of things, including a wife who they say was very beautiful. Then he had an accident.'

'What kind of accident?'

'He drove a fast sports car. One day he was with his wife. They were on their way to Palermo. Around Misilmeri a little girl of five dashed across the road. She was killed instantly. He was stunned, froze like a statue, and didn't know what was happening. The car kept on going, ran off the road and off a cliff. He broke three ribs and his left arm, but his wife died in hospital four days later. And from that moment, his life changed.'

'Was he convicted?'

'Yeah, but nothing serious. There were witnesses who said that even if he'd been doing fifty the little girl would still have been run over.'

'In what sense did his life change?'

'He sold almost everything he owned and started doing charity work. He kept only a country cottage and a place here in town. He's a truly devout man.'

'So, in conclusion, it was a waste of time.'

'No, Chief, it wasn't a waste of time, because we've still eliminated one of the four names.'

He looked down at his toecaps and asked: 'Did you call La Cosulich last night?'

'Yes. She gave me two names.'

Now it was the inspector's turn to take a piece of paper out of his pocket. He handed it to Fazio.

'Pennino, to take revenge on Cosulich, closed his accounts with the Banca Siculo-Americana and accused her, to the manager, of having mistreated him.'

'I know this Pennino,' said Fazio.

'And what's he like?'

'I think the man is capable of anything.'

'Apparently he's even someone who sends anonymous letters.'

Fazio pricked up his ears.

'If La Cosulich could let us see one . . .'

'You want to compare it with the ones Mr Z has sent us, right?'

'Right.'

'Sorry to disappoint you. Cosulich had one but threw it away. Listen, I don't want to burden you with too much work. I'll look into Pennino and Parisi myself.'

He wrote down the names and addresses of Pennino and Parisi on another scrap of paper and sent for Catarella.

'Listen, Cat, send a fax to Montelusa Central, internal offices. I want to know if they've ever investigated either of these two men, if they have any ongoing, or if they are planning to start any.'

'Straightaways, Chief.'

Montalbano spent an hour signing papers, then massaged his arm and went out to eat.

＊

'Enzo, please give this packet back to the young lady, when she comes for it this evening.'

Enzo didn't venture to say anything.

And as he was making this definitive gesture, Montalbano was instantly overcome by a werewolf-like hunger.

Even Enzo was impressed.

'Enjoy it in good health, Inspector.'

This time he took his walk along the jetty at a fast pace, practically running, not the usual one foot up, one foot down. And when he reached the lighthouse, he deemed it insufficient.

And so he turned around and did it all over again.

At last, panting heavily, he sat down on the flat rock and lit a cigarette.

'I made it,' he said to the crab huddling motionless on the green slime and looking at him quizzically.

*

'Ah, Chief! Jess now a 'spector jess like you called from Montelusa!'

'Did he give you his name?'

'Wait a secon', I writ it down 'ere on a piss o' paper.' He found it and looked at it.

' 'Z name's Pisquanelli.'

'Pasquarelli, Cat.'

He was chief of the drugs squad.

'An' wha'd I say?'

Better drop it.

'What did he want?'

''E says as how y' oughter go 'n' see 'im, 'im meanin' the forementioned Pasquanini, as soon as possibly possible, cuz 'arse wha'ss best f'r 'im.'

'For him meaning Pasquarelli?'

'No, Chief, f'r 'im meanin' yiz.'

Since he didn't have anything urgent on his plate, he was better off killing some time going to Montelusa than signing papers in his office.

'I'll go right now.'

He got back in his car and drove off.

*

Pasquarelli was someone who did his job well and therefore was much to Montalbano's liking.

'Why are you interested in Michele Pennino?' he asked as soon as Montalbano came in.

'And why are you interested to know why I'm interested in Pennino?'

Pasquarelli laughed.

'OK, Salvo, I'll go first. But I should inform you that I've already talked about it with the commissioner and he acknowledged that I'm in charge.'

'In charge of what?'

'Of Pennino.'

'Then there's no point in my wasting any time here.'

'Come on, Salvo, we have a mutual respect for each other and so there's no reason for us to make war. Why are you interested in him?'

'I think he may be leading a burglary ring in Vigàta that has—'

'I've heard mention of it. It couldn't possibly be him.'

'Why not?'

'Because we've had him under strict surveillance for the past month and a half.'

'Drugs?'

'We're almost certain that Savino Imperatore, who was the biggest importer in the province, was replaced after his death by none other than Pennino. I can assure you, Salvo — I can guarantee it, in fact, with a twist of lemon on top — that Pennino is not the man you're looking for.'

'OK, thanks,' said the inspector. And he left.

*

'Ah, Chief, Chief! Ahh, Chief!'

This was the heartrending lament that Catarella typically voiced when hizzoner Mr C'mishner called.

'Wha'd he want?'

''E said, 'e bein' 'im, the beforementioned Mr C'mish'ner, 'e said 'e wants 'a see yiz immidiotwise straightaways an' oigently oigentwise wittout a minnit's dillay!'

But he'd just got back from Montelusa!

Spouting a litany of curses, he got back in his car.

*

He had to wait forty-five minutes in the waiting room before the commissioner would see him.

'Please come in and sit down.'

Montalbano gave a start. The commissioner asked him to sit down? What was happening? Was the world coming to an end?

Then there was a light knock at the door. 'Come in,' said the commissioner.

The door opened and Deputy Commissioner Ermanno Macannuco appeared.

He was almost six and a half feet tall, conceited and off-putting, and carried his head the way priests carry the sacrament in processions.

He'd been at the job in Montelusa for barely four months, but that had been more than long enough for Montalbano to grasp that the man was a certified cretin.

The commissioner asked him to sit down. Macannuco didn't say hello to Montalbano, and the inspector likewise pretended he hadn't seen him.

'You do the talking,' said Commissioner Bonetti-Alderighi.

Macannuco talked, but looked only at the commissioner the whole time, and never at Montalbano.

'. . . I raised the point that any eventual investigation on the part of the Vigàta police must be halted because it interferes.'

'Interferes with what?' Montalbano asked the commissioner, who didn't reply but only looked at Macannuco.

Who said: 'With a preceding investigation.'

Montalbano decided he would have some fun. He made a bewildered face.

'And what is a receding investigation?'

'He didn't say "receding" but "preceding",' the commissioner clarified.

'I beg your pardon, but according to the *Rigattini-Fanfani* dictionary, not to mention the *Devoto-Oli*, "preceding" means something that's already happened. Now, if the investigation of Parisi was conducted in the past by Commissioner Macannuco, I don't see how a new investigation on my part could possibly—'

'For heaven's sake, Montalbano, let's not start splitting hairs!' the commissioner chided him.

'I used "preceding" in the sense of "prior",' Macannuco specified with a sneer.

'But prior to now, I have not conducted any investigations whatsoever into Parisi!' the inspector protested.

'It's what we're doing!' Macannuco exclaimed.

'For what reason?'

'Pietro Parisi is a known paedophile at the head of a network extending all across Italy.'

'But wasn't his name Eugenio? Precedingly, I mean,' Montalbano asked, with a cherubic face.

'What kind of idiocies is he saying?' an irritated Macannuco asked the commissioner in turn. 'The man I'm investigating is called Pietro.'

'And mine is Eugenio.'

'That's not possible!' yelled Macannuco.

'I swear to you it is!' said Montalbano, standing up and holding up his right hand as if in court.

'Perhaps a little check is in order?' the commissioner suggested paternally to Macannuco.

The deputy commissioner stuck a hand in his pocket, pulled out a sheet of paper, unfolded it, read it, turned pale, stood up, and bowed to the commissioner.

'My apologies, I've made a mistake.'

And he walked out strutting like a turkeycock.

'I'm sorry we wasted your time,' the commissioner said to Montalbano.

'Not at all!' Montalbano said magnanimously. 'It's always a pleasure to see you!'

*

On his way back to Vigàta, he decided to go and talk to Parisi at once.

He invented an excuse. He would tell him that Angelica Cosulich had reported him, and that they'd done an analysis of the anonymous letter, and his handwriting had appeared to match it.

In short, he would fire a shot in the dark in the hope of hitting something.

He remembered that Via del Gambero was in the neighbourhood of the harbour. He was right.

Number 21 was a huge apartment building with a doorman.

'Eugenio Parisi?'

'He's not here.'

'What do you mean, "He's not here"?'

'I mean exactly what I said.'

What was happening to all the doormen in Vigàta? 'But does he live here?'

'As for living here, he lives here.'

Montalbano lost his patience.

'I'm Inspector Montalbano!'

'And I'm the doorman Sciabica.'

'Tell me what floor he lives on.'

'Top floor, eighth floor.'

Montalbano headed towards the lift. 'Lift's out of order,' the doorman shouted. Montalbano did an immediate about-turn.

'And why did you say he's not here?'

''Cause he's in Palermo, in the hospital. His wife's there too.'

'Since when?'

'About two months.'

'Thanks.'

'You're welcome.'

Another dead end.

*

He was parking the car at the station when he saw Catarella shoot out of the building like a rocket and come running towards him. He was waving his arms in the air as if to signal that he had big news.

'Ahh, Chief Chief Chief!'

This meant something even bigger than a phone call from the commissioner.

'What's up?'

'Anutter buggery!'

'Where?'

'Onna street called Mazzini, nummer 41.'

In the same neighbourhood as the Peritores and Cosulich.

'Who called to report it?'

'Summon sez 'is name is Pirretta.'

Antonino Pirrera! Number nine on the list! 'When did he call?'

''Roun' five-toity.'

'Where's Fazio?'

''E's awreddy onna scene.'

*

Fazio was standing outside the main door of Via Mazzini 41 and talking to someone.

In this case the architect had designed a two-family house, though in the style of a chalet in the Bavarian Alps.

With steeply pitched roofs to avoid the accumulation of snow which had never, in human memory, fallen in Vigàta.

'How did they do it?' Montalbano asked Fazio.

'This gentleman is the doorman of the building next door.'

The doorman held out his hand.

'Ugo Foscolo,' the man said, introducing himself.

'I'm sorry, but were you by any chance born in Zakynthos?' Montalbano asked him.

'Tell the inspector what happened,' said Fazio.

FOURTEEN

'Around four o'clock this afternoon, a small truck pulled up in front of my building and the driver called out to me. He said they had to adjust the Pirreras' satellite dish, which is on the roof of number 41.'

'Tell me exactly what they wanted from you.'

'Well, since they knew I had the keys to number 41 . . .'

'Why do you have them?'

'It's just a two-storey house, right? On the ground floor you've got Mr and Mrs Tallarita, who go out every day at seven in the morning and come back at five-thirty in the evening. The Pirreras, who live upstairs from them, go out at eight, come back for lunch, then go out again, then the wife comes back around five-thirty, while the husband doesn't usually come home until after eight. An' that's why they leave me the keys to the front door, just in case.'

'And what did those people want?'

'They wanted me to open the front door and then the little door to the staircase leading to the roof.'

'And did you do it?'

'Yessir.'

'Did you wait around until they'd finished their work?'

'No, sir, I went back to my porter's lodge.'

'And what happened next?'

'About three hours later, they came back down, thanked me, and told me they'd finished. And I went and locked up again.'

'How many of them were there?'

'Three.'

'Did you get a good look at their faces?'

'I got a good look at two of them, but not the other one.'

'Why not?'

'He was wearing a cap and a scarf that covered his face up to his nose. He had a cold and was coughing.'

'Thank you. You can go now.'

'Now tell me the rest,' Montalbano said to Fazio.

'Well, the three men went up on the roof, broke through the skylight, went into the Pirreras' apartment, and headed straight for the safe. Which they opened, and that was that. Which is why I called Forensics.'

'You did the right thing. What does Mr Pirrera do?'

'He has a jeweller's shop, which he runs with his wife. The man is desperate.'

'And did they steal anything else from the apartment?'

'Apparently not.'

'Did Arquà come along with his men?'

'Yes, sir.'

Arquà was chief of the Forensics lab, and Montalbano couldn't stand him. The feeling was mutual.

'Listen, I'm going home. Call me later with the whole story.'

'All right.'

'Oh, and I wanted to tell you I found out about Pennino and Parisi. Pennino is being watched by the drugs squad, and Parisi's been in a hospital in Palermo for the last two months.'

'So La Cosulich was wrong?'

'So it seems. And you can lift the night-time surveillance of the residences. We've lost the game.' He turned around, took three steps, then came back. 'Have the doorman come in to the station tomorrow morning. He got a good look at two of the men's faces. Show him the picture files. I'm not expecting him to recognize anybody, but it has to be done.'

✻

Back at home he undressed and got into the shower, hoping it would have a calming effect. All this going back and forth to Montelusa, and now the burglary and the sense of having lost the game, had put him in an agitated state.

So Mr Z had done it!

He'd changed his method completely, and it had worked!

He'd kept his word. One had to grant him that. And he'd made Montalbano look like a dickhead. The inspector didn't even feel like going to see what Adelina had made him for dinner.

He just sat out on the veranda feeling powerless and angry.

By now it was clear. He had to look reality in the face. It was time to retire.

*

Fazio's phone call came half an hour later.

'Chief, Pirrera's on his way to the station to file a report. But what I really wanted to tell you is that Forensics may have discovered something important.'

'Namely?'

'They found a key up on the roof, a car key. They think one of the burglars dropped it. They rule out any possibility that it was there before.'

'Are there any fingerprints on it?'

'No. And there weren't any on the safe, either. I also wanted to tell you a rumour I heard.'

'Tell me.'

'Actually it wasn't so much a rumour as a chorus of rumours. Apparently Pirrera is a loan shark.'

'A good thing to know. Who's got the key?'

'I do.'

'I'll be right over.'

'What for?'

'I'll tell you when I get there.'

That key, for him, was like a raft in a shipwreck.

✳

'Has Mr Pirrera left?'

'Just now.'

'You worked fast.'

'He came with the list already drawn up. A jeweller knows what he's got in his safe.'

'Good. Have you got all the phone numbers of the people on the list?'

'Yes, sir.'

'How many men have you got here at the station right now?'

'Five.'

'Keep 'em here. Now call all those people. Get Catarella and a few others to help you.'

'What should I say?'

'That I want them all there, at the station, in an hour, with every car they own.'

'Chief, in an hour it'll be eleven p.m.'

'So what?'

'Maybe some of them have already gone to bed . . .'

'If they've gone to bed, they'll have to get up.'

'And what if somebody refuses?'

'You'll tell them you have orders to bring them in in handcuffs if they refuse.'

'Chief, be careful what you do.'

'What do you mean?'

'These are rich people, Chief. They've got powerful friends they can complain to, and they can do you harm . . .'

'I don't give a fuck.'

He'd suddenly become the Montalbano of old again.

'We'll proceed as follows. As the people arrive, they must leave their cars in the car park, unlocked, with the keys inside, and come into the waiting room. I don't want them to see what we're doing in the car park. Is that clear?'

'Perfectly.'

✫

He stayed for more than an hour at the window, smoking one cigarette after another.

Then Fazio came in.

'They're all here, except for Mr and Mrs Camera, whom I was totally unable to get in touch with. And you know what? We've had a stroke of luck.'

'How?'

'Ten of them had got together for a game of bridge. They're all in a bad mood and demanding an explanation.'

'And we'll give them one. You got the key from Forensics?'

'In my pocket.'

'How many cars are there?'

'Twenty-four. Some of them own more than one.'

'Start checking.'

✶

When he got to his sixteenth cigarette, his throat was parched and the tip of his tongue burned.

Fazio burst in with a triumphant air.

'The key belongs to Tavella the accountant's car, no doubt about it!'

'I would have bet the family jewels on it,' said Montalbano.

Fazio gave him a puzzled look. 'You mean you already knew?'

'Yes, but not in the way you're thinking.'

'And what do we do now?'

'Send them all home with our heartfelt apologies. Except for La Cosulich, Tavella, and Maniace.'

'And why not just Tavella?'

'Because it's better to blow a little smoke in their eyes. After they're all gone, come back here with Cosulich. But be careful. Post a guard in the waiting room. Neither Tavella nor Maniace must be allowed to leave. For any reason.'

Five minutes later Angelica stood before him, accompanied by Fazio.

'Have a seat, both of you.'

They both sat down in the chairs in front of the desk.

The first thing Montalbano noticed was that Angelica's wonderful sky-blue eyes seemed to have lost their colour.

'I apologize for having detained you, signorina. But it was just to tell you that we've thoroughly investigated the two names you were so kind to give us. Unfortunately neither of the two could have written the anonymous letter.'

Angelica shrugged, indifferent.

'It was just conjecture on my part.'

Montalbano stood up, and she did likewise. He held out his hand to her.

Angelica's hand felt cold.

'Goodbye. Fazio, please see the young lady out and then ask Mr Maniace to come in.'

'Goodbye,' Angelica said without looking at him.

With Maniace he would have to invent the first thing that came into his head.

'Good evening,' said Maniace, coming in.

'Good evening.' Montalbano replied, getting up and extending his hand. 'Please sit down. This should only take a few seconds.'

'I'm glad to be of help.'

'A certain Davide Marcantonio claims to have been a

business associate of yours ten years ago in a funeral-home venture. Now, since Marcantonio is accused of—'

'Just a minute,' Maniace interrupted him. 'I don't know anyone by the name of Marcantonio and I've never had a funeral home.'

'Really? Were you born in Pietraperzia?'

'No, in Vigàta.'

'Then this must be a case of mistaken identity. I'm terribly sorry. Have a good evening. Fazio, please show the gentleman out.'

Fazio came back like a rocket. 'Should I go and call Tavella?'

'No, let him stew in his own juices a little. He's seen that we dealt with La Cosulich and Maniace in a few seconds. And now he's wondering why we're not calling him. The more nervous he gets, the better.'

'Chief, could you explain to me how you thought of him right away?'

'You told me that Tavella was drowning in debt because of his gambling addiction. And you also told me that Pirrera was a loan shark. What's in the basket?'

'Ricotta,' said Fazio.

'And that's what they want us to think. Whereas, in this particular basket, there's no ricotta but something else.'

Fazio leapt up in his chair. 'So you think that . . .'

'. . . that Tavella is the perfect scapegoat. But I could be wrong. Are there any bars open at this hour?'

'In the immediate neighbourhood, no. But if you just want a coffee, Catarella has a machine. It's pretty good.'

*

After the coffee, Montalbano told Fazio to go and get Tavella.

He was a man of about forty, slender, well dressed, with curly hair, glasses, and a few slight tics.

'Please sit down, Mr Tavella. I'm sorry to make you wait, but I had to verify a few things first.'

Tavella sat down and adjusted the creases on his trousers. Then he touched his left ear twice.

'I don't understand why—'

'You'll understand soon enough. And please have the courtesy to refrain from making comments. Just answer my questions, and we'll be done with this all the sooner. Where are the keys to your car?'

'This gentleman here told us we had to—'

'Ah, yes. Fazio, go and get them.'

Before leaving, Fazio looked at him, and Montalbano looked back. They immediately understood each other.

'Where do you work, Mr Tavella?'

'At the town hall, in the property office. I'm an accountant.'

'Did you go to work this afternoon?'

'No.'

'Why not?'

'I was given permission to take the afternoon off to give my wife a hand at home. This evening all our friends were coming over for our weekly game of bridge.'

'I see.'

Fazio returned with the keys. There were two of them, attached to a metal ring.

He put them down on the desk.

'Have a good look at them, sir. Are those your car keys?'

'Yes.'

'Are you sure?'

Tavella stood up halfway from his chair to look at them more closely.

He touched his left ear twice. 'Yes, those are mine.'

'One is for the ignition, and the other's for the boot, correct?'

'Correct.'

'Now, can you explain to me why this ignition key doesn't have your fingerprints on it?'

Tavella was stunned. He opened and closed his mouth. He felt an urgent need to adjust the crease in his trousers. And to touch his left ear four times.

'That's not possible! How could I have come here without using my key?'

'By using a different key. Put it on the desk, Fazio.'

Fazio put on his gloves, pulled out a plastic bag, took the key from it, and put it down on the desk beside the other two.

'The one you see here on the key ring was put there by Fazio before you came in.'

'I'm not understanding anything any more,' said Tavella, touching his left ear eight times. 'So how is it you have this other key of mine?'

'It was found on the roof of the Pirreras' building, which was burgled today. Which I'm sure you know about.'

Tavella turned as pale as a corpse. Then he leapt to his feet, trembling all over.

'It wasn't me! I swear! My spare keys are at home!'

'Please sit down. And try to stay calm. Where do you keep them?'

'Hanging on a hook near the front door.'

Montalbano held out the telephone to him. 'Does your wife drive?'

'No.'

'Then call her and ask her if the spare set of keys is still there.'

Tavella's hands were trembling so badly, he misdialled the number twice. Fazio intervened, while the accountant's ear was being massacred.

'What's the number?'

Tavella told him, and Fazio dialled it and passed him the receiver.

'Hello, Ernestina? No, nothing's happened, I'm still at the police station. Just a slight misunderstanding, it's nothing. Yes, I'm fine, there's nothing to worry about. But I want you to do me a little favour. Go and see if the spare set of car keys is in the usual place.'

Tavella's forehead was drenched in sweat. His left ear had turned redder than a red pepper.

'They're not? Did you have a good look? OK, thanks, I'll see you later.'

He put the receiver down and threw up his hands, dejected.

'I don't know what to say.'

'So therefore you don't know how long they've been missing.'

'But I wasn't paying any attention! They were there, with the others, the keys to the attic, the keys to the cellar . . .'

'Please answer me sincerely.'

'And what have I been doing up to now?'

'Do you owe Pirrera money?'

Tavella didn't hesitate for a second. 'Yes. It's no secret, everybody knows!'

'Do your friends know?'

'Of course!'

'How much do you owe?'

'It started out as a hundred thousand euros, and now that's become five hundred thousand.'

'So Pirrera's a loan shark?'

'You be the judge. He's been sucking the blood of half the people in town for thirty years!'

A tremendous, inexplicable – or perhaps all too explicable – weariness suddenly came over the inspector. 'Mr Tavella, unfortunately I have no choice but to detain you.'

The poor man buried his face in his hands and started crying.

'Believe me, I have no choice. You have no alibi, your car key was found at the scene of the crime, and you have a plausible motive for detesting Pirrera . . .'

The inspector's anger at having to follow abstract rules, and the sorrow he felt for this poor man who surely considered himself innocent, made him feel sick.

'You can tell your wife now, if you like. And tomorrow you can call your lawyer. Fazio, please take care of things.'

He dashed out of the room, as if he might suffocate if he stayed in his office for another second.

Passing in front of Catarella, he noticed he was still engrossed in the computer.

'Still playing the same game?'

'Yeah, Chief.'

'How's it going?'

'Bad. Bu' my partner, 'oo's me m'sself, 'z comin' a help.'

Something inside the inspector began to rebel.

Why on earth did he have to go exactly by the book?

When had he ever done so before?

He dashed back into his office.

Fazio's hand was on the receiver, and he was about to call the accountant's wife.

Tavella was still crying.

'Fazio, let me have a word with you.'

Fazio joined him in the hallway.

'I'm going to send the man home.'

'OK, but . . .'

'I want you to write a report saying our holding cell is not usable due to prior flooding.'

'But it hasn't rained for a month!'

'That's precisely why it's "prior".'

Montalbano went inside.

'Mr Tavella, I'm going to let you go home to your wife, but I want you here tomorrow morning at nine with your lawyer.'

He left the room before the stunned Tavella could start thanking him.

FIFTEEN

His appetite was completely gone.

He set himself up on the veranda in the usual fashion. By now it was clear that Mr Z was one of the names on the list.

He not only knew the life story of everyone on the list, but also their habits and daily routines.

It was anybody's guess how long ago Mr Z had got his hands on Tavella's keys. Probably one evening when he'd gone there to play bridge!

But why had Mr Z – who, if he really was one of the names on the list, was a man above suspicion and fairly well off – decided to become the leader of a burglary ring?

In an anonymous letter, he'd written that he didn't touch any of the loot from the robberies, leaving it all to his accomplices.

So why did he do it? For fun? Right!

Clearly he was looking for something that was of great importance to him.

And he'd found it, if the burglaries were over now.

Mr Z wasn't looking for something random, but for something in particular.

And therefore he knew where this thing was.

The only burglary that Mr Z was really interested in was the last one, of the Pirrera home.

To the point that he'd planted evidence against Tavella.

Which was a sort of curtain falling at the end of the performance.

All the previous burglaries had only served to pay the work of the gang. And to throw the police off the trail.

Was it possible Mr Z, like Tavella, owed money to Pirrera?

Or did Pirrera have something of interest to Mr Z in his safe?

And there were other considerations concerning Mr Z to be made as well.

All the people on the list had known one another for years and spent time together.

Why did Mr Z suddenly decide to start robbing his friends at a particular moment, and not before or after?

What triggered this chain of events?

What new development had led him to become a criminal?

Also: how had he known how to get in touch with a

gang of burglars? It's not like they're out for hire on the open market; it's not as if you can just go to the employment exchange and say: 'Excuse me, I need three expert burglars.'

At any rate, he resolved to call Pirrera in the morning and squeeze him hard.

＊

He'd just lain down in bed when his thoughts turned back to Angelica.

There was something in her composure, when he'd informed her that Pennino and Parisi had nothing to do with the anonymous letter, that had struck him.

She'd remained completely indifferent.

Whereas he'd been expecting another reaction entirely.

Angelica had seemed spent, burned out, to him.

It was as though the whole affair had nothing to do with her any more.

Maybe the bank's management had decided to transfer her after all?

＊

At last he fell asleep.

But he slept for barely half an hour before he suddenly woke up.

A sharp, troubling thought had come into his mind and prevented him from sleeping.

No, it wasn't a thought, but an image.

What was it?

He strained his brain trying to remember.

Then it came back to him.

Catarella in his cupboard, playing his computer game. What did that have to do with anything?

Then he remembered perfectly how Catarella had explained the game:

The game cossitts o' doin' a most damage y' can do to the apposing couple, who'd be the avversary, bu' also tryin' a proteck y'r own partner from danger.

What did it mean?

In some obscure way he sensed that these words were very important.

But in regard to what?

He racked his brains till daybreak.

Then, at the break of dawn, a little light entered his brain as well.

And he shut his eyes at once, as if to keep that light out.

It really hurt, that light.

It was like a knife blade stabbing him painfully in the heart.

No. It wasn't possible. And yet . . .

No, it was absurd to think such things! And yet . . .

He got up, unable to stay in bed any longer.

Mygodmygodmygodmygodmygod . . .

Was he praying?

He put on his trunks.

He opened the French windows to the veranda.

Mygodmygodmygodmygodmygod . . .

The early morning fisherman hadn't arrived yet. The air was cool. It gave him goose bumps.

He went down to the beach and dived into the water. So much the better if he got a cramp and drowned.

Mygodmygodmygodmygodmygodmygod . . .

*

He went into the kitchen, still dripping wet, made his usual mug of black coffee, and drank the whole thing.

The ringing of the telephone was like a burst of machine-gun fire.

He looked at his watch. Barely six-thirty.

'Chief? Fazio here.'

'What is it?'

'A murder.'

'Where?'

'Along an unmade road in the Bellagamba district.'

'And where's that?'

'If you want I'll come and pick you up.'

'All right.'

*

He decided not to tell Fazio about the unbearable thought he'd had. First he needed positive confirmation.

'Who reported it?'

'A peasant whose name Catarella didn't quite get.'

'Did he give any details?'

'Nothing. He said the body was in a ditch next to a large boulder with a black cross painted on it.'

'Did Catarella tell the man to wait for us?'

'Yes, sir.'

✻

They found the boulder with the black cross on it without a problem.

All around was utter desolation. Not a single house to be found anywhere, but only clumps of sorghum and wild weeds as far as the eye could see, and a few sickly trees. The only living beings were grasshoppers as big as your finger and flies in such dense swarms that they looked like black veils in the air. Not even dogs barking.

Most importantly, the man who'd found the body wasn't there either.

Fazio pulled up, and they got out of the car.

'The man's gone,' said Fazio. 'He did his duty but doesn't want any trouble.'

The dead man was in a ditch that ran alongside the road.

He lay belly-up, eyes wide open and mouth twisted into a sort of grimace.

He was bare-chested, had a great deal of hair on his chest and arms, but still had his trousers and shoes on. No visible tattoos.

Montalbano and Fazio crouched down to have a better look.

He was about forty, with a few days' stubble on his face.

They could see two wounds, despite the million and more flies swarming around them.

The left shoulder was bluish and puffy.

Fazio put on some plastic gloves, lay down with his stomach on the ground, and gently turned the body over. 'The bullet must still be in his body. But the wound is infected.'

The other wound had devastated his neck.

'That's an exit wound, on the other hand,' said the inspector. 'They must have shot him from behind, through the base of the skull.'

Fazio repeated the operation. 'You're right.'

He then stuck his hand under the corpse's pelvis. 'There's no wallet in the back pocket. Maybe he kept it in his jacket. In my opinion he's been dead for a few days already.'

'I agree.'

Montalbano heaved a long sigh. Now began the

tremendous pain in the arse of the prosecutor, the Forensics team, the coroner . . . He wanted to get out of that
depressing place as soon as possible.

'All right, go ahead and call the circus. I'll keep you
company until they get here, but then I'm leaving. Tavella's
coming in this morning.'

'Oh, right. Ugo Foscolo's coming too – you know, the
doorman – to see if he recognizes . . .'

Montalbano had a flash of inspiration. With nothing
to justify it.

'Have you got his phone number?'

'Whose?'

'Foscolo's.'

'I do.'

'Call him at once, tell him to come here, and let him
have a look at the corpse.'

Fazio looked perplexed.

'Chief, what makes you think—'

'I don't know. It's just something that came into my
head, but we've got nothing to lose by trying.'

Fazio made the phone calls he had to make.

But another hour passed before Dr Pasquano, the
coroner, arrived.

The doctor looked around.

'Nice place, here. Really cheerful. They never leave us
a body, say, in a discotheque or an amusement park . . . I
wonder why that is? . . . Looks like I'm the first here.'

'Unfortunately.'

'Jesus fucking Christ, I spent the whole night at the club and I'm so tired it's eating my flesh . . .' Pasquano exclaimed in irritation.

'Did you lose?'

'Mind your own damn business,' the doctor replied in his customary gentlemanly way.

Apparently he'd lost. And badly.

'And when do you think his honour the prosecutor will deign to arrive?'

'He was the first one I called,' said Fazio, 'and he said he'd be here in an hour at the most.'

'If he doesn't crash into a telephone pole first,' said Pasquano, growing more and more agitated.

It was well known that Prosecutor Tommaseo drove worse than a hippie on LSD.

'Have a look at the body in the meantime,' Montalbano suggested.

'Go and look at it yourself. I'm going to catch up on my sleep for a couple of hours,' said the doctor.

And he climbed into the hearse, throwing out the two stretcher-bearers.

'Just take my car,' said Fazio. 'I can go back with one of them.'

'See you later.'

✳

'Ahh, Chief! I wannit a tell yiz 'at 'ere's summon inna wait-in' room waitin' f' yiz poissonally.'

'Tavella.'

'Nossir, iss Trivella.'

'OK, send him in to me.'

Tavella was considerably less agitated than the day before. In fact, he touched his ear only once. Apparently he'd recovered from the terrible blow of the unexpected false accusation.

'I wanted first to thank you for being so understand-ing—'

Montalbano cut him off.

'Did you call your lawyer? Did you speak to him?'

'Yes, but he can't come for another half-hour.'

'Then go back to the waiting room, and let me know when he gets here.'

The inspector rang Prosecutor Catanzaro on the direct line. He was the one in charge of burglaries and robberies.

They were fond of each other and addressed each other informally.

'Montalbano here. Have you got fifteen minutes to spend on the phone?'

'Let's make that ten.'

He told him all about the burglaries and Tavella. 'Write me up a report, and in the meantime send Tavella and his lawyer to me,' Catanzaro said in the end.

With saintly patience, Montalbano started to write the report, which he would have Catarella copy afterwards.

Half an hour later, Catarella called to say the lawyer had arrived.

'Send him in.'

He dispensed with him in five minutes, sending them both to Catanzaro's office.

It took him another half-hour to finish the report, which he handed over to Catarella to type into the computer.

Then he rang Fazio. 'How are things going?'

'Chief, Prosecutor Tommaseo ran into a cow.'

Now that was something new. Tommaseo had already crashed into just about everything – trees, letter boxes, poles, milestones, trucks, flocks of sheep, and tanks – but never into a cow.

'Did Foscolo come?'

'Yeah, but he didn't recognize the body.'

Too bad. The inspiration hadn't been very inspired. 'So you've got enough to keep you busy all morning?'

'So it seems.'

'And what's Pasquano doing?'

'Luckily he's asleep.'

✻

Around one o'clock, as he was about to go out to eat, he rang Tavella.

'The prosecutor put me under house arrest for now. But I swear, Inspector, I nev—'

'You don't have to swear to anything, I believe you. You'll see, it'll all turn out all right.'

☆

He left the office and went to Enzo's trattoria, but ate lightly.

After his usual walk along the jetty, he returned to the station.

Fazio was there waiting for him. 'What did Pasquano say?'

'He wouldn't let anyone get near him, let alone ask him anything. He was so infuriated it was frightening . . .'

'I'll give him a ring this evening. But I already know what he's going to say.'

'And what's that?'

'That the first wound, the one in the shoulder, was inflicted some forty-eight hours before the shot to the neck that killed him.'

'And who shot him?'

'The first shot? Can't you guess?'

'No, sir.'

'Our very own Loschiavo.'

'Holy shit!'

'Calm down. He only wounded him, in self-defence. I'll write the report for the commissioner myself.'

'So how did it happen, in your opinion?'

'Well, during the shoot-out at the Sciortinos' beach house, Loschiavo wounds one of the burglars. The bullet remains in his shoulder, but his accomplices don't know how to treat him, and they can hardly take him to the hospital. Then the wound gets infected, and his friends, to avoid complications, decide to kill him. We'll know whether I'm right or not when Pasquano extracts the bullet.'

'I think you're right,' said Fazio.

'Therefore this man died before the Pirrera house was burgled,' the inspector continued.

'That's clear.'

'But there were still three burglars. That's what Foscolo said.'

'Right.'

'Which can mean only one thing. That Mr Z decided to take part in the burglary in person, taking the dead man's place. He must be the man in the cap and scarf who was pretending he had a cold.'

'That seems likely. But in so doing he took a huge risk.'

'It was worth it.'

'In what sense?'

'I've come to the conclusion that the only burglary Mr Z was really interested in was this last one. The previous ones served only to pay the members of the ring and also to

muddy the waters. There was definitely something in Pirrera's safe other than jewellery. This thing is now in Mr Z's
hands, and you can be sure we won't be hearing about this
burglary ring any more. But I'm convinced there will soon
be consequences. I'm expecting some sort of fireworks.'

'Really? But that leaves us empty-handed.'

'There may still be a way . . .'

'Then tell me what it is.'

'You should keep digging for information on those
three names from the list I gave you the other day, but while
you're digging, I want you to find whatever excuse you can
to go and see the widow Cannavaro again, the busybody.'

'What do you want to know?'

'Look, Fazio, my hunch is flimsier than a spider's
thread, but we can't ignore it. You have to try and find out
if anything new or unusual happened within the Peritores'
circle of friends about three or four months ago.'

'What sort of new or unusual thing?'

'I have no idea. But just have her tell you everything
she knows. Squeeze her dry.'

'All right, I'll get on it right away.'

Less than twenty minutes later, Fazio rang. 'The
widow's gone to see her son in Palermo.'

'Do you know when she'll be back?'

'The doorman says late tomorrow morning.'

*

Just before eight o'clock, he picked up the phone and called Dr Pasquano.

'What's the story, Doctor?'

'You decide. Will it be Little Red Riding Hood? The Fable of the Transformed Son? Or just a little joke? Do you know the one about the doctor and the nurse?'

'Please, Doctor, it's late, and I'm tired.'

'Ah, I see. And I'm not?'

'Doctor, I merely wanted to know——'

'I know exactly what you wanted to know. And I'm not going to tell you, OK? You can wait for the report.'

'But why are you so spiteful today?'

'Because I've had it.'

'Can I ask just one question?'

'Only one?'

'Only one. Word of honour.'

'Ha ha ha! Don't make me laugh! Only men give their word of honour. And you're not a man, but a wreck! Why don't you resign? Don't you realize how decrepit you are?'

'Got it all out of your system, Doctor?'

'Yes. Now ask me your damn question and then go and retire to an old people's home.'

'Aside from the fact that you're older than I am and could never retire to an old people's home because you couldn't pay the bills since you lost all your money playing poker, the question is as follows: did you remove the bullet from the man's shoulder?'

'Now I've got you! Got a guilty conscience, have we?'

'Why do you say that?'

'Because you cops shoot at people without a second thought!'

That was what he wanted to know.

'Thank you for your exquisite courtesy, Doctor. And I wish you the very best of luck at the club tonight.'

'Oh, fuck off!'

SIXTEEN

He didn't feel like going home.

Because it would have meant being alone.

And being alone would have meant starting to think again about the idea he'd had the previous night.

Which had made him feel really bad.

So, dear Montalbano, are you a coward? Don't have the courage to face the situation?

I never said I was a hero, he answered himself. *Anyway, nobody likes performing hara-kiri.*

He decided to eat at Enzo's.

'What's wrong, is Adelina on strike?'

'No, I left what she made for me in the oven too long and it burned.'

Lies, as usual. Whatever the circumstance. Lies. He told them, and they were told to him.

'Ah, Inspector, I almost forgot. I wanted to tell you

that the young lady still hasn't come by to pick up that packet you left.'

And why was that? Had she forgotten? Or had she far more serious things to think about?

'Let me have it.'

'I'll get it right away.'

He didn't know where that command had come from. Certainly not from his brain.

Enzo brought the packet, and Montalbano put it in his jacket pocket.

What was he going to do with it? He didn't know.

'So, what'll you have?' Enzo asked.

✳

He ate a lot, and slowly, to make the time pass.

Afterwards, he went to the movies.

'But the last show began ten minutes ago, Inspector.'

'It doesn't matter.'

Those ten minutes lost at the beginning of the movie, which was about espionage, were probably crucial, since he didn't understand a damn thing about the rest.

When he came out it was twelve-thirty.

He got in his car, and his hand on the steering wheel took him in the direction of Via Costantino Nigra.

Like the last time, he parked outside the service entrance at the back of the ice-cream-cone-shaped building.

What was he doing there? He didn't know. He was just following his instincts. Reason had nothing to do with it.

There wasn't anyone around. He got out, crossed the street, opened the door, and closed it behind him.

Inside, everything was exactly the same as before. He got into the lift and pressed the button for the last floor from the top.

He climbed the stairs, trying to make as little noise as possible.

He pressed his ear to the door.

At first he didn't hear anything, only his racing heart. Then, as though far away, he heard Angelica speaking loudly.

Moments later he realized there was nobody there with her, and she was talking on the phone.

And since her voice sounded at times closer and other times further away, he guessed she was talking on her mobile phone and walking from room to room.

Then he heard her very close by. She was upset, almost hysterical.

'No! No! I've always told you everything! I haven't hidden anything from you! What reason would I have for keeping something so important from you? Do you believe me or don't you? Well, then I think I'll just hang up! Good night!'

She must have done so, since Montalbano now heard her crying disconsolately.

For a moment he was tempted to unlock the door, rush in, and comfort her.

But he had the strength to turn tail and head for the staircase.

*

When he got back to Marinella, it was past one o'clock.

He got undressed, put on his trunks, went down to the beach, and started running along the water's edge.

An hour and a half later he fell face-down on the sand and remained there.

After a short spell he summoned the energy to run home at the same pace.

When he lay down in bed, exhausted, it was four o'clock in the morning.

He was dead tired and utterly incapable of thought. He'd achieved his purpose.

*

'You wanna some caffee, sir?'

'What time is it?'

'Almos' nine.'

'Bring me one later.'

No! No! I've always told you everything! I haven't hidden anything from you! What reason would I have for keeping something so important from you?

It might mean everything, or it might mean nothing.

After drinking his coffee, he showered. Then he heard Adelina outside the bathroom door.

'Tiliphone for you, sir.'

'Who is it?'

'Catarella.'

'Tell him I'll call back in five minutes.'

He got ready in a hurry, driven by the premonition that after the death of the burglar something had changed, and that there would be consequences, even if he didn't know what kind.

'Cat, Montalbano here.'

'Ahh, Chief! Mr Pirrera committed sluicide!'

'Who reported it?'

''Is wife.'

'Has Fazio been informed?'

'Yessir. Since 'e did it at 'is jewry shop in Via de Carlis, 'arse where Fazio is.'

He must mean Via de Carolis. 'I'm on my way.'

*

Fazio was waiting for him outside the half-lowered metal shutter.

Four busybodies were talking softly a short distance away.

News of the suicide hadn't spread yet. The local TV news reporters and cameramen didn't know anything about it.

'Did he shoot himself?'

Normally jewellers always have a gun within reach. And they end up creating havoc by shooting at would-be thieves.

'No, Chief, he hung himself in the back room.'

'Who found him?'

'His wife, poor thing. But she summoned the strength to tell me Pirrera got here two hours earlier than usual this morning. Said he had to put his registers in order. The wife came in around quarter to nine as usual, only to find him in the back room.'

'Is she inside now?'

'The wife? No, Chief. She was in a pretty bad way, so I had an ambulance take her in to Montelusa Hospital.'

'Did he leave any kind of written statement?'

'Yes, a piece of paper with one line on it: *I am paying for what I've done.* And his signature. Want to have a look at it?'

'No. Have you called the circus?'

'Yes, I have, Chief.'

What was he still doing there? 'I'm going to the office.'

*

All in all, he could consider himself satisfied, even though having his hunch confirmed by a suicide wasn't actually cause for great satisfaction.

Mr Z had most certainly found what he was looking for in Pirrera's safe.

That is, the proof of what Pirrera had done. But what had Pirrera done?

Or: why did Mr Z want what he was looking for? Knowing this would solve everything.

*

'Are you sure it was a suicide?' Montalbano asked Fazio when he returned to headquarters.

'Absolutely. Forensics took the suicide note anyway, for a handwriting analysis. But I want to say something. Do you remember I put Caruana on the tail of de Martino the engineer?'

'Yes.'

'I told Caruana not to bother any more. By now it seems pretty clear to me that de Martino's got nothing to do with the burglaries.'

'You're right. So where do things stand with the other names?'

'Chief, between burglaries and deaths it's not like I've had a lot of time on my hands. But we can cross another name off the list.'

'Which one?'

'Francesco Costa.' The ignorant one with no professional titles. 'He's practically a midget, and so—'

'So what? Are you saying a midget can't—'

'Let me finish. Ugo Foscolo gave me a thorough

description of the burglars, and none of them was particularly short.'

'OK, you're right.'

'And he can't be Mr Z, either, because you pointed out, correctly, that Mr Z took part in the last burglary.'

'Right again. So that leaves two names, for now. Schirò and Schisa. Get back to work.'

✳

It took him over an hour to write his report on the exchange of fire outside the Sciortinos' house. He wanted to make sure that Loschiavo's actions appeared unimpeachable.

When he was done, he brought it to Catarella.

Then he went back into his office, and before he had even sat down, the phone rang.

'Ah, Chief! 'At'd be a jinnelman onna line 'at I can't unnastan' 'ow 'e talks!'

'So why do you want to put him through to me?'

'Cuz th' only woid I c'd unnastan' f' sher was yer name annatt'd mean yiz.'

'But did he tell you what his name was?'

'Nah, Chief, 'e din't.'

It wasn't as if he had a lot to do, so he might as well. 'OK, put him through.'

'Inspector Montalbano?' The voice sounded muffled, strange.

'Yes, who's this?'

He distinctly heard the man take a deep breath before speaking.

'Listen to me carefully. You can consider Miss Cosulich as good as dead.'

'Hello? Who—'

The other hung up.

Montalbano turned to ice.

Then the feeling of cold turned to heat, and he began to sweat profusely.

The voice of the man on the phone had clearly been distorted on purpose.

The message left no room for doubt, unfortunately. But why did they want to kill her?

No! No! I've always told you everything! I haven't hidden anything from you! What reason would I have for keeping something so important from you?

Those were not words addressed to a jealous lover. But what sense did it make for them to take the trouble of informing him of all people, a police inspector, of their murder plans?

Didn't they realize that he would immediately put Angelica under police protection?

And that he would do everything within his power to prevent this pre-announced murder?

A hypothesis that might seem at first glance demented began to make its way into his head.

What if the man who had phoned actually wanted to achieve the opposite result?

Say Angelica was threatened for something she did. Or didn't do.

If the reason for which she was threatened was something that couldn't be revealed, she certainly couldn't come to the police and report the threat.

And so her friend intervenes and makes the phone call to Montalbano.

That way, the police must necessarily protect her.

If things indeed were as he imagined them, then there was only one thing he could do.

'Catarella, get Fazio for me.'

He had to wait five minutes before Fazio answered.

'There's a new development. Can you come here right away?'

'I could, but I'm being told something important right now.'

'When do you think you'll finish?'

'In about an hour.'

'I'll wait for you.'

'Catarella!'

'Yessir, Chief!'

'Call the Banca Siculo-Americana and ask to speak with Miss Cosulich. But don't tell them you're with the police.'

Catarella said nothing. Apparently the inspector's prohibition had thrown his brain into confusion.

'So 'oo's I asposta say 'z doin' na talkin'?'

'Say you're the secretary of the Bishop of Montelusa. As soon as she comes to the phone, say: "Please wait, I'm putting you in direct communication with His Excellency," and then put me on.'

'Jeez, 'at's wunnafull!'

'What's wonderful?'

'This fack!'

'What fact?'

'Since whenna ya bin made a ixcillincy?'

'Cat, His Excellency is the bishop!'

'Oh!' said Catarella, disappointed.

Montalbano had time to review the six times table before the telephone rang.

'Hello?' said Angelica.

Montalbano put down the receiver.

That was all he'd wanted to know. As long as the girl was inside the bank, she was safe.

'Catarella!'

'Yessir, Chief.'

'Call Montelusa Hospital and ask if Mrs Pirrera can receive any visitors.'

'Shou' I still say iss 'is ixcillincy the bishop?'

'No, in fact you should say the call is from the Vigàta police.'

✳

Going into a hospital as a healthy man always made him feel uneasy.

'Who are you looking for?' a rather severe-looking woman asked him from behind a desk in the entrance.

'Mrs Pirrera?'

The woman consulted the computer in front of her.

'You can't see her without the doctor's permission.'

'Let me speak to the doctor.'

'Are you a relative of the patient?'

'I'm her blood brother.'

'Please wait a moment.'

The sourpuss got on the phone. 'He's on his way.'

Some ten minutes later a very thin man of about forty in glasses and a white smock appeared.

'I'm Dr Zirretta. And who would you be?'

'There's no "would be" about it: I'm Inspector Montalbano, of that I'm absolutely certain.'

The man looked at him in dismay.

'I need to talk to Mrs Pirrera.'

'She's sedated at the moment,' said the doctor.

'Do you understand or don't you?'

'Yes, I do, but I can only allow you five minutes. Go ahead and talk to her. She's on the second floor, room twenty.'

For some reason, the inspector always got lost in hospitals. This time was no exception.

In the end, when he finally found the room some ten

minutes later, there was Dr Zirretta standing outside the door.

'The five minutes start now,' the inspector said to him.

There were two beds in the room, but one was empty.

Mrs Pirrera was about fifty, rather plain and fat, and very pale.

Her eyes were closed. Perhaps she was sleeping. Montalbano sat down in the chair beside her bed.

'Mrs Pirrera.'

The woman opened her eyes slowly, as though her eyelids weighed a ton.

'I'm Inspector Montalbano, of the Vigàta police. Do you feel up to answering two or three questions?'

'Yes.'

'Do you have any idea why your husband . . .'

She threw her hands up in the air.

'I just can't . . .'

'Listen, was your husband greatly affected by the robbery?'

'He went crazy.'

'Was there a lot of jewellery in the safe?'

'Probably.'

'I'm sorry, but hadn't you seen what was in the safe?'

'He never wanted me to.'

'One last question, and then I'll let you rest. After the robbery, did your husband receive any letters or phone calls that—'

'That same evening. A phone call. A long one.'

'Do you know what it was about?'

'No. He sent me into the kitchen. But afterwards . . .'

'Was he worried, frightened, upset?'

'Frightened.'

'Thank you, signora.'

Now it all made sense.

Mr Z had used what he'd found in the safe to black-mail Pirrera.

Or perhaps drive him to suicide.

✧

Fazio was at the station.

'Sorry, Chief, but when you called I was talking with the widow Cannavò.'

'What did she tell you?'

'This time she was fixated on her friends' illnesses. One man had pneumonia, and some lady had rheumatism, and so on. She filled my ears with useless chatter. But she did reveal that Schisa swings back and forth from depression to mania and probably spent a year in a mental hospital, in her opinion.'

'And this is supposed to be important?'

'Well, Chief, it's obvious that Mr Z's mode of behaviour isn't exactly normal.'

'Indeed . . . What about this idea of some new development within the group?'

'Nothing, Chief. She swore there was nothing new that happened within the group. Or that if there was, she hadn't noticed.'

Another dead end.

'What did you want to tell me?' Fazio asked.

'Something rather curious. I got a call from a man who told me I should consider La Cosulich as good as dead.'

An electric shock seemed to pass through Fazio's body.

'Are you kidding me?'

'Come on!'

Fazio remained silent for a moment, reflecting.

Every so often he shook his head as if to say 'no'. Then he spoke.

'Well, it seems pretty strange to me for someone to call the police when he's about to kill someone.'

'Well done! That's exactly what I thought.'

'And were you able to work out what he was trying to achieve with that phone call?'

'The exact opposite of what he was saying.'

SEVENTEEN

'Meaning what?' Fazio asked, puzzled.

'He wanted complete protection for the girl.'

'And who would threaten to kill her?'

'Bah! . . . Who knows . . . The only way to find out is to talk to her. Call her at the bank and tell her to come here this afternoon, when she gets off work.'

'Who's going to talk to her, you or me?'

'We'll both talk to her. Now listen up.'

'Go ahead.'

'Knowing your secret vice of collecting people's personal details, I'm sure you know everything about the people on the Peritores' list. Their fathers' and mothers' names, places of birth, family relations . . .'

Fazio blushed. 'Well, yes, I do.'

'Do you have this information here at the station?'

'Well, yes, I do.'

'Bring it to me and then go and make that call.'

Fazio returned five minutes later with two sheets of paper in his hand.

'I called her; she'll be here at seven. And here's that information.'

'I'll look at it later. Now it's time for lunch.'

✲

After eating, while sitting and smoking on the flat rock under the lighthouse, his thoughts turned to Angelica again.

And he thought of the bitter conclusion he'd reached that terrible night when he'd ruminated over the game Catarella was playing on the computer.

A conclusion he'd pushed away with all his might, but which he could no longer shunt aside.

The moment of truth had come. It could not be put off any longer.

He saw a man walking along the jetty and heading towards where he was.

Maybe he was coming to do maintenance work on the lighthouse.

Then he heard the sound of diesel motors coming from the mouth of the port.

He turned around to look.

It was a fishing trawler returning at an odd hour. It must have had engine problems, because the sound it made was uneven.

Not a single seagull was following it.

Once upon a time there would have been at least ten behind it.

But nowadays seagulls no longer hung around by the sea; they were in town, on rooftops, stooping to look for food in rubbish bins, alongside the rats.

Sometimes, at night, he heard their angry, desperate cries . . .

'Inspector . . .'

He jerked his head around. It was Fazio.

He'd seen him but not recognized him. He jumped to his feet.

His eyes looked deep into Fazio's.

His brain roared with a sound like a giant wave.

In a flash he understood why Fazio was there in front of him, pale-faced in spite of the sun and the walk he'd just taken.

'Is she dead?'

'No, but she's in a grave condition.'

Montalbano did not so much sit back down as collapse onto the rock.

Fazio sat down beside him and put his arm around him. A sort of terrible wind was raging inside the inspector's head, preventing his thoughts from forming, from linking together. They were like so many fallen leaves scattered in every direction by the wind – indeed, they weren't thoughts at all, but fragments, bits, images that lasted a second and then were swept away and vanished.

Montalbano brought a hand to his head, as if it could somehow stop that chaotic, uncontrollable motion.

Mygodmygodmygodmygodmygod . . .

That was all he was able to say, a sort of refrain that wasn't a prayer but a kind of entreaty, though soundless, without moving his lips.

He was suffering like an animal wounded in a sudden ambush. He wished he could become a crab and run and hide in a hole in a rock.

Then, little by little, that storm, the same way as it had started, began to die down.

Nostrils dilated, he breathed in the sea air deeply. Fazio, worried, did not take his eyes off him.

After a short while, the inspector's brain started working again, but still not the rest of his body.

He felt a kind of dull oppression around his heart, and knew that if he tried to stand up, his legs would not be able to bear his weight.

He opened his mouth to speak but couldn't. His throat was all dried up, as though burned . . .

Then he removed Fazio's arm from around his shoulders, leaned his whole body over, at the risk of falling into the sea, and managed to touch the water. He thrust his hand into it and wet his lips, licking them with his tongue.

Now he could talk. 'When did it happen?'

'After everyone left the bank for lunch at one-thirty. Since the restaurant is nearby, they always walk there.'

'Have you seen her?'

'Yes, as soon as the call came in to the station and I realized what was going on, I raced over there.'

'And . . . you saw her?'

'Yes.'

'And how was she?'

'Chief, she was shot square in the chest. Luckily there was a doctor there who staunched the wound.'

Montalbano had trouble asking the question again. 'Yes, but how was she? Was she suffering a lot? Was she crying?'

'No. She was unconscious.'

He breathed a sigh of relief. So much the better. Now he felt in a condition to carry on.

'Were there witnesses?'

'Yes.'

'Are they at the station?'

'Yes. Actually I had only one come in, the one who seemed the most precise.'

'Why didn't you inform me at once, before rushing to the scene? You could have come to get me or called me at Enzo's.'

'What good would that have done? And anyway . . .'

'Anyway what?'

'It didn't seem like a good idea. I wanted first to be sure she was still alive.'

He felt certain that Fazio had sensed there was something between him and Angelica.

And he got confirmation of this at once. Fazio cleared his throat.

'If you want me to call Inspector Augello . . .'

'Why would I want you to do that?'

'To get him to come back.'

'But why?'

'In case you don't feel like taking this case . . .' Fazio felt clearly uneasy.

'I feel like it, don't you worry about that. I have to feel like it, I have no choice. It was due to a failure on my part that they—'

'Chief, nobody could have known—'

'I should have known, Fazio. I should have known, can't you see that? And after the anonymous telephone call I shouldn't have left her unprotected for even a minute.'

Fazio remained silent. Then he said:

'Want me to drive you to Montelusa Hospital?'

'No.'

He wouldn't have been able to bear seeing her lying there unconscious in a hospital bed. But perhaps he'd said 'no' too decisively, too resolutely, because Fazio gave him a confused look.

'Instead, try and find out how she is and whether they've operated on her.'

Fazio stood up and took a few steps away.

He spoke on his mobile phone for what seemed to the inspector like an eternity. Then he returned.

'The operation was successful. She's in the recovery room. But they can't change their guarded prognosis for another twenty-four hours. They can't say whether or not she's out of danger yet.'

Now the inspector was certain his legs would hold up. 'Let's go back to the office,' he said.

But in order to walk he had to lean on Fazio's arm.

*

'Let me talk to the witness.'

'He's an accountant who works with Cosulich; his name's Gianni Falletta. I'll go get him.'

Falletta was a rather elegant young man of about thirty, with blond hair and an intelligent look about him.

Montalbano had him sit down. Fazio, who was going to type up the exchange for the report, asked Falletta for his personal particulars. Then the inspector joined in.

'Tell us how it happened.'

'Well, we'd all gone out together to go to the restaurant. Since it's not very far, we always walk there. Angelica was walking by herself, a little ahead of the group.'

'Did she normally do that? Wasn't she part of the group?'

'Yes, she was, but she got a call on her mobile and instinctively started walking ahead.'

'OK, continue.'

'We turned off the main street and rounded the corner

onto the street with the restaurant at the far end. All of a sudden we heard the rumble of a large motorcycle behind us. We all stepped to the right to let it pass, and I noticed that Angelica had done the same.'

'Excuse me for interrupting, but you seem to have had your eye particularly on Miss Cosulich.'

Falletta blushed.

'Not really . . . but, you know how it is . . . Angelica's such a beautiful girl . . .'

He could say that again! 'Go on.'

'The motorcycle wasn't going particularly fast . . . actually it was going rather slowly . . . And so it drove past our group, past Angelica, and at that moment, the man riding on the back—'

'There were two men on the motorcycle?'

'Yes, two. And at that moment, the man on the back turned round and fired.'

'One shot?'

'Two.'

Montalbano looked questioningly at Fazio, who gave a nod as if to say yes.

'And then the motorcycle immediately accelerated and was gone,' the accountant concluded.

'Were you able to get a look at the face of the man who fired the shots?'

'Are you kidding? Both were wearing helmets that entirely covered their faces. But, in a way, Angelica was lucky.'

'What do you mean?'

'I distinctly saw – just as the man was extending his arm to shoot – I saw the motorcycle lurch violently; it must have hit a pothole or something. And so the first shot missed, but the second hit her in the middle of the chest. I'm sure he was aiming straight at her heart.'

'Did you manage to get a look at the licence plate?'

'No.'

'None of you saw it?'

'No, none of us. I wasn't thinking . . . Anyway, after they shot her, you can imagine what happened. Everybody ran in every direction . . . And it just didn't occur to me to look at the licence plate . . .'

'Why not?'

'My first thought was . . . Well, I just ran towards Angelica, who was lying in the middle of the street.'

'Did she manage to say anything?'

'No. I bent down over her, she was white as a sheet, her eyes were closed, she seemed to have trouble breathing . . . that horrific red stain on her blouse was growing and growing . . . I was about to pick her up off the ground when a man looking out from a balcony above said not to, and said he'd be down right away. He's a doctor who has his office there. He'd already called an ambulance, but when he came down he immediately started to staunch the wound.'

'Thank you, Mr Falletta.'

'Can I say something?'

'Of course.'

'In the last few days poor Angelica wasn't . . . well, she wasn't her usual self.'

'And how was she?'

'I don't know . . . very nervous . . . sometimes even rude . . . as if her thoughts were always elsewhere, always focused on something . . . well, unpleasant. You see, Inspector, ever since Miss Cosulich arrived at the bank about six months ago, the atmosphere had changed . . . it had become more cheerful . . . more liveable . . . Angelica has a smile that . . .'

He stopped. Up to that point he'd been able to control himself, but suddenly his lips began to tremble, at the memory of Angelica's smile.

And Montalbano realized that young Falletta, the accountant, was hopelessly in love with her too.

He felt sorry for him.

*

When Fazio returned from having seen Falletta out, Montalbano asked him what had happened to the mobile phone.

'You mean Angelica's? When the ambulance arrived, it ran over it and smashed it into a thousand pieces. What's worse, most of the pieces fell into a drain.'

'Why didn't you think to grab it at once?'

'Because I didn't find out Angelica had been on the phone until after the ambulance arrived. It was too late. The damage was already done.'

Montalbano picked up the receiver.

'Catarella? Get the manager of the Banca Siculo-Americana on the line and then put him through to me.'

'His name's Filippone,' Fazio informed him, 'and he's a rather nasty sort. One of the employees had run back to tell him what had happened, and he raced to the scene. And then—'

'Why, he doesn't eat with the others?'

'No, he just eats a little bit of fruit in his office. Anyway, he raced to the scene, and while they were waiting for the ambulance to arrive, all he could do was repeat that the whole episode would damage the bank's reputation.'

The telephone rang. Montalbano turned on the speakerphone.

'Mr Filippone? This is Inspector Montalbano, of the Vigàta police.'

'Good afternoon, what can I do for you?'

'I need some information.'

'Banking information?'

'I'm sorry, but if I call a bank, what kind of information am I going to ask for? About the latest outbreak of the flu in Malaysia?'

'No, but, you see, we are held to the rules of banking secrecy. And our manner of procedure, moreover, is one of transparency, in full, absolute respect of the prerogatives of—'

'I want a list of all your clients, and I want it at once. That's not a secret.'

'Why do you want it?' Filippone asked, alarmed.

'Because. You know, we, too, are required to maintain investigative secrecy.'

'Investigative?' asked Filippone, scared to death. 'Listen, Inspector, I don't think the telephone is the proper venue for discussing—'

'Then come here to the station. And make it snappy.'

Fazio smiled at him.

'You're making him pay for it, eh?'

*

Filippone came in sweaty and out of breath.

He was a man of about fifty, chubby, pink-skinned, and almost beardless, perhaps distantly related to some forgotten breed of swine.

'Do not think for an instant that I wish in any way to obstruct . . .' he said, sitting down with great dignity.

'I don't think,' said Montalbano. 'Fazio, do you think I could think such a thing?'

'I don't think so,' said Fazio.

'You see? Now, just a few questions for the purpose of the investigation. Is there anyone among your customers who belongs to the Cuffaro family?'

'I don't understand what you mean by your use of the word "family".'

'How long have you been the manager of your branch of the Banca Siculo-Americana?'

'Two years.'

'Are you Sicilian?'

'Yes.'

'Then don't tell me you don't know the meaning of the word "family" down here.'

'Well . . . I don't have any of the Cuffaros as customers.'

The other Mafia family in Vigàta was the Sinagra clan.

'What about the Sinagras?'

Filippone wiped the sweat from his brow.

'Well, there's Ernesto Ficarra, who's a nephew of—'

'I know who he is.'

Montalbano pretended to write something down. 'How much credit are you exposed for with him?'

Filippone blanched. The sweat was now pouring down his face in rivulets. 'How did you know?'

'We know everything,' said the inspector, who had fired a shot in the dark and been right on target. 'Please answer my question.'

'Er . . . well, a lot.'

'Are you aware that Ernesto Ficarra is currently awaiting trial on racketeering charges, wholesale drug trafficking, and pimping?'

'Well, a few rumours had reached my—'

'A few rumours! And this is your famous transparency?'

Filippone was now drenched.

'A final question, and then you can do me a favour and get the hell out of here. Is one of your customers a man by the name of Michele Pennino?'

Filippone livened up slightly. 'Not any more.'

'Why not?'

'Well . . . for no reason he decided to withdraw his—'

'For no reason? Do you know you're taking a very big risk by not telling me the truth?'

Filippone deflated like a punctured balloon.

'He had asked Miss Cosulich not to . . . not to be so formal about the declarations as to the provenance of the sums Mr Pennino was depositing . . .'

'But one day Miss Cosulich rebelled and refused to accept Pennino's deposit, and he changed banks. Is that what happened?'

'Yes.'

'Now get out of here.'

*

'So you think it was Pennino who—'

'Not in my wildest dreams. I just wanted to know whether Angelica gave me Pennino's and Parisi's names just to throw me off the trail. I took a roundabout path with

the bank manager because I wanted to frighten and con-
fuse him.'

'Whereas Cosulich told you the truth.'

'Only in part,' Montalbano admitted.

Fazio opened his mouth but then closed it immediately.

'Meanwhile,' the inspector continued, 'there's no
longer any need for you to keep trying to find out whether
anything unusual happened within the Peritores' circle a
few months ago.'

'Why not?'

'Because Falletta's already told us.'

'Falletta?! How?'

'The unusual thing happened when Cosulich moved to
Vigàta six months ago. She may have already told me this,
but I'd forgotten it. Now we need to find out who it was
that introduced her immediately into that circle. It's
extremely important.'

Fazio remained silent for a long time.

Then he spoke, looking down at his toecaps. 'Chief,
when are you going to make up your mind and tell me
what you know or think about Miss Cosulich?

Montalbano had been waiting for this question for
quite some time.

'Soon. For now bring me the information on the last
name, Schirò. I'm going home; I feel tired. I'll see you in
the morning.'

EIGHTEEN

He sat out on the veranda, not having eaten. His stomach was tight as a knot, as if in the grip of a closed fist.

> 'Alas!' he said, 'my heart both burns and freezes,
> Now that my love is rendered null and void.
> What shall I do? . . .'

No, enough of Ariosto. Above all, enough of the Angelica of his youth. There was only one thing to be done; there was no point in continually asking himself. And that was to proceed straight ahead, even if it cost him a great deal, or too much.

He pulled out of his pocket the two sheets of paper Fazio had given him with the personal particulars. He'd taken them on his way out of the office and now settled in to study them.

But even he didn't know what he was looking for. Then he stopped short.

Because inside his brain, some of Angelica's words had suddenly come back to him.

. . . my mother was from Vigàta . . . my father's no longer around either . . . a terrible accident, here . . . I was only five at the time . . .

A sort of wave of heat came over him, so strong that he had to get up at once and have a shower.

When he was done, he went back out on the veranda and read Angelica's personal particulars.

Angelica Cosulich, daughter of Dario Cosulich and Clementina Baio, born 6 September 1979, and residing in . . .

Feeling suddenly restless, he got up and phoned police headquarters.

'Yer orders, Chief.'

'Listen, Cat, do you feel like working tonight?'

'I c'd woik a tousand nights f' yiz, Chief!'

'Thanks. The archive of *Il Giornale dell'Isola* has all been computerized, hasn't it?'

'Yessir. We awreddy consalted it once.'

'OK, I want you to search the year 1984 and see if you can find a report on a traffic accident in which two people lost their lives, a husband and wife, whose names were – now write this down correctly – Dario Cosulich and Clementina Baio. Now repeat them back to me.'

'Vario Cosulicchio 'n' Clementina Pario.'

'Let me dictate them to you again. Try to get it right

this time. And as soon as you've found the article, call me back at home.'

*

Good thing the night was beautiful, relaxing, and quiet.

Montalbano needed only look out at the sea and sky to feel his agitation diminish a few degrees.

He was on his sixth glass of whisky and had just opened his second pack of cigarettes when the phone rang.

'I foun' it, Chief, I foun' it! I foun' it an' I prinnit it!'

Catarella was triumphant.

'Read it to me.'

Catarella started reading.

> *Vigàta, 3 October 1984. From our correspondent.*
>
> This morning the lifeless bodies of Dario Cosulich, aged forty-five, and his wife, Clementina Baio, aged forty, were found at their home at Via Rosolino Pilo 104, by the cleaning woman. The apparent causes of death are murder and suicide.
>
> After killing his wife with one gunshot, Mr Cosulich turned the weapon on himself. Dario Cosulich, a native of Trieste, moved to Vigàta seven years ago, where he opened a wholesale fabric shop. After a successful start, business began to go bad. One week before the tragic

event, Mr Cosulich was forced to declare bank-
ruptcy. The motive of jealousy in the
murder-suicide has been ruled out. Apparently
Mr Cosulich could no longer meet the exorbitant
demands of the illegal lenders from whom he
had borrowed money.

All that was missing was the final piece of the mosaic
he could now see clearly before his eyes. He went back out
onto the veranda and resumed reading the pages with the
personal details.

And he noticed at once that his eyelids were drooping.
But when he reached the eleventh name, that of Ettore
Schisa, on the second page, he felt a sort of electric shock
run through his body.

So he went back and reread the names on the first
page.

And all of a sudden he realized that he might well
have found the final piece he was looking for.

Angelica Cosulich, daughter of Dario Cosulich
and Clementina Baio, born on 6 September
1979, and residing in Vigàta at Via . . .

Ettore Schisa, son of Emanuele Schisa and
Francesca Baio, born in Vigàta on 13 February
1975, and residing in Vigàta at Via . . .

It was only a minimal point of contact, of course, and
might, under examination, prove entirely random.

Maybe Fazio, with Schisa, had guessed right.

He looked at his watch. It was past one o'clock. Too late for anything.

Suddenly, from the sea, a voice.

'Inspector Montalbano!' it shouted. 'Go to bed!'

It must have been someone on a boat, messing around. In the dark he couldn't see anything. He stood up.

'Thanks!' he shouted back. 'I'm taking your advice!' And he went to bed.

*

The phone woke him at eight. It was Fazio. 'Morning, Chief. I just wanted to tell you that I talked to a friend who works at the hospital. Miss Cosulich had a good night, and the doctors are amazed at her quick recovery.'

'Thanks for calling. Where are you?'

'At the office.'

'Those sheets of paper you gave me with the personal particulars, are they the originals or a copy?'

'They're copies. I've got the originals here.'

'Have you had any time to look at them?'

'No.'

'Then look at them now and compare the info on Cosulich with that on Schisa.'

'Holy shit!' Fazio exclaimed a moment later.

'Now, while I'm washing and getting dressed, I want you to put your records-office genius to work. OK?'

'All right. I'll go straight to the town hall.'

'Oh, and, on your way out, ask Catarella for the article he read to me last night, and have a look at it yourself.'

*

Two mugsful of coffee made him fully lucid again. It was going to be a rough day. He found Fazio at headquarters. 'I went to the Registry Office. Clementina and Francesca Baio were sisters. So what do we do now?'

'Now we proceed according to the script. We go and pay a call on Dr Ettore Schisa.'

'Sorry for asking, Chief, but wouldn't it be better if we informed the prosecutor first?'

'It'd be better, but I don't feel like wasting any time. I want to get this business over with as quickly as possible. Let's go. Have you got a pocket tape recorder?'

'Yes, I'll go and get it.'

*

Fazio pulled up in front of Via Risorgimento 48.

It was a four-storey building, a bit run-down. 'Schisa lives on the second floor,' said Fazio.

They went in through the front door. There was no porter or lift.

As they climbed the stairs, Fazio took out his revolver, stuck it into his waistband, and buttoned up his jacket. Montalbano gave him a strange look.

'Don't forget the man's half crazy, Chief.'

Fazio rang the doorbell. Moments later, the door opened.

'Dr Ettore Schisa?' Montalbano asked.

'Yes.'

The inspector couldn't believe his eyes.

Schisa wasn't even thirty-five years old, and yet the man who stood before him looked at least fifty, and didn't even wear those fifty well.

Unkempt, shod in slippers, unshaven, dishevelled, wearing a shirt that he clearly hadn't changed for days, with a dark, greasy ring around the collar.

He had a gleam in his eyes like someone ill or on drugs. And the bluish circles under them seemed painted on, making him look strangely like a clown.

'I'm Inspector Montalbano, police, and this is Inspector Fazio.'

'Please come in,' said Schisa, standing aside.

They went inside. Montalbano immediately noticed that the air in the apartment was sickly, heavy, irrespirable. There wasn't a hint of order in any of the very large rooms. On their way to the living room, Montalbano saw a dish with leftovers of pasta on a chair in the hallway, a pair of socks on a small table, as well as trousers, books, shirts, glasses, bottles, and dirty coffee cups scattered all over the floor.

Schisa told them to sit down. Before he could settle

into an armchair, Montalbano had to remove a pair of cheesy, used underpants that lay on top of it. Fazio, in turn, removed an ashtray that was overflowing with cigarette butts.

'Dr Schisa,' the inspector began, 'we're here to—'

'I know why you're here,' Schisa interrupted him.

Montalbano and Fazio exchanged a quick glance.

'Then you tell us,' said the inspector.

'May I turn on the tape recorder?' Fazio asked.

'Yes. You came about the burglaries.'

Schisa lit a cigarette. Montalbano noticed that his hands were shaking.

'You guessed right,' said the inspector.

Schisa stood up.

'I don't want to waste any of your time. Now if you'd be so kind as to follow me . . .'

They followed him.

He stopped in front of the door of the last room in a long corridor, opened it, turned on the light, and went inside.

'Here are the stolen goods. It's all here, nothing's missing.'

Montalbano and Fazio were astonished. They hadn't expected this.

'So what you wrote in your note wasn't true?' the inspector asked.

'No. I paid off the three men handsomely, in cash,

after each burglary. They would make an estimate of the value, which I would then pay. I cleaned myself out; haven't got a penny left.'

'Where did you find the money?'

'My income as a doctor would never have allowed me to amass the money I needed. Some years ago I won a lot betting on football and I put it aside.'

'Mind if I have a look around?' asked Fazio.

'Go right ahead.'

Fazio entered the room, bending down to look at all the stuff scattered randomly everywhere. The stolen paintings were hanging on the walls.

'The jewellery and furs belonging to Miss Cosulich seem to be missing,' Fazio said after finishing his inspection.

'They're missing because they were never stolen. In fact they never existed,' said Schisa.

'That robbery was supposed to serve as cover for Miss Cosulich, wasn't it?' Montalbano asked.

'Exactly. Shall we go back to the living room?'

They returned to their former places.

'Now I'll ask the questions,' said the inspector. 'You, Dr Schisa, planned a series of burglaries to throw us off the trail of the only one you were really interested in: Pirrera's. What was in that safe?'

'Pirrera was a loathsome loan shark without a scrupulous bone in his body. He has ruined dozens of families. Including Angelica's and my own.'

'Why your own?'

'Because my father and Dario Cosulich had married the Baio sisters. And my father was Dario's business associate in the fabric shop. Uncle Dario killed his wife and then himself, and my father died of a broken heart two years later. Ever since, my only thought has been to avenge them.'

'Answer my question: what was in the safe?'

'Two Super 8 movie reels. And some photographs. When his victims ran out of money, he would demand payment in kind. The films show Pirrera in action with two little girls, one seven and the other nine years old. Would you like to see them?'

'No,' Montalbano said, grimacing. 'But how did you ever find out about them?'

'Pirrera used to get his jollies showing them to the wretched women he forced to sleep with him. I was able to track down one of these women, and I paid her to give me a written description.'

'When did you make the decision to take revenge?'

'When I became a legal adult. I'd been thinking about it all along, but didn't know how to go about it.'

'Was it the arrival of your cousin Angelica that—'

'Yes. The whole thing came to a head when Angelica was transferred here. We talked about it for whole nights at a time. At first she resisted the idea; she was against it, but then, little by little, I managed to persuade her.'

'How did you go about recruiting the burglars?'

'I knew that Angelica . . . well, that every now and then she got together with . . .'

'I know everything,' said Montalbano.

'Anyway, I suggested that she try to find, among the men she encountered, someone who would be willing to . . . And then one day she ran into the right man. Angelo Tumminello. The one who was wounded by one of your officers and whom the other two ended up killing.'

'Could you tell me the names of Tumminello's two associates?'

'Of course. Their names are Salvatore Geloso and Vito Indelicato. They're both from Sicudiana.'

Fazio wrote the names down on a scrap of paper. 'Now tell me why the two men shot Miss Cosulich.'

'That's a more complicated matter. You see, after you went to Angelica's place following the burglary, she told me, in the presence of the other three, that you and she had become friends. To the point that she agreed not to talk about the burglary in the room that she had in her cousin's villa.'

'Wait a second,' the inspector interrupted him. 'You used to meet there to organize the burglaries?'

'Yes. And so Tumminello suggested that she hook up with you so that we could know your moves in advance.'

Fazio was studying the floor tiles and didn't dare raise his head.

'When you told her you'd be out personally watching the Sciortinos' house, I suggested she go and join you. Which she agreed to do. Except that she called us shortly afterwards and said that you'd phoned her and told her that the stakeout had been cancelled. Is that true?'

Fazio jerked his head up and looked at him. Montalbano was taken by surprise, but quickly recovered himself as bells began to ring joyfully in his head.

'Yes, it's true,' he said. It was a whopper as big as a house, but at that point . . .

'But when the three men fell into the trap and Tumminello was wounded, the other two became convinced that Angelica had betrayed them,' Schisa continued.

'When you wrote in your anonymous letter about some unforeseen factor, were you referring to Angelica's possible betrayal?'

'Yes.'

'So, like your accomplices, you no longer trusted her?'

'Well, at first I was torn. Then I became convinced that Angelica had not betrayed us. I phoned her and she sounded sincere. I told the others, but . . .'

'About the anonymous letters. In the first one, where you were trying to get me into trouble, you didn't reveal the real purpose for which Angelica used that room. Why not?'

'I had no interest in exposing her or creating problems for her. On the contrary, I had to protect her.'

As in Catarella's game. He'd guessed right. 'Go on.'

'There's not much else to say. I tried to convince them that they were wrong, but it was no use.'

'Was it you who called me and disguised your voice, to alert me to the mortal danger Miss Cosulich was in?'

'Yes, I thought it was a good idea, but those cretins found a way to shoot her just the same.'

'Did you personally take part in the Pirrera robbery?'

'Tumminello had been killed by then. I had no choice. Otherwise all my work would have gone down the drain with his death.'

'When you got your hands on those films and photographs, did you call Pirrera immediately?'

'I called him the very evening of the burglary. And I told him I would be sending everything anonymously to you, Inspector, the following day.'

'Did you know what would be the outcome of your telephone call?'

'Of course! I was counting on him killing himself! I was burning with hope! I prayed to God he would do it! And he did it, the swine!'

He started laughing.

And he didn't stop. It was a terrible scene.

He rolled on the floor, laughing. He hit his head against the wall, laughing.

After a while he started frothing at the mouth, and Fazio made up his mind. He approached and punched him hard on the chin. Schisa collapsed, unconscious, and Fazio got on his mobile phone to ask for reinforcements. The whole apartment needed to be searched and inventoried. In short, there was a lot of work to be done.

'Call a doctor, while you're at it,' Montalbano suggested.

Indeed Schisa, when he came to, started laughing and drooling again.

He was unable to remain standing, and when they sat him down he spilled onto the floor as though made of jelly.

The inspector realized that it was unlikely Schisa would ever return to normal. Something seemed to have broken inside him. For years the desire for revenge had eaten him up inside, and now that he'd achieved his goal, his whole body – brain, nerves, muscles – seemed to have come apart.

The doctor came in an ambulance and took him away. Not until Fazio had found the Super 8 reels and photographs did Montalbano leave the apartment. Meanwhile he'd found a snapshot of Angelica with Schisa and put it in his pocket.

He got into his car and went to talk to Tommaseo. He told him everything, emphasizing in particular that all the stolen goods had been recovered, that Schisa was out of his mind, that at any rate he hadn't killed anybody, that he had good reasons for wanting to avenge himself, and that Angelica had been entirely coerced by her cousin.

Prosecutor Tommaseo put out an order for the immediate arrest of Geloso and Indelicato. Then, with keen
interest, he asked:

'What's the woman like?'

Without saying a word Montalbano dug the snapshot
out of his pocket and handed it to him.

Tommaseo lost his head over every pretty girl he saw.

And the poor man was not known to have ever had
any female friends.

'Jesus!' the prosecutor said, drooling worse than Schisa.

✻

When the inspector got back to Vigàta, it was already past
two o'clock. He had no appetite, but went for a walk
along the jetty just the same.

Now that he'd done just about everything he had to do
– though the hardest part was yet to come – there was
only one thought spinning around in his head.

Still the same one.

He sat down on the flat rock.

> *Sitting on a rock, gazing at the sea,*
> *Immobile as a rock itself would be.*

Stock-still, with only one thought in his head.

> *Angelica did not betray me.*

But he couldn't tell whether this thought gave him
pleasure or caused him pain.

He wished he never had to go back to the station. And he cursed his life as a policeman a thousand times.

But what had to be done, had to be done.

'I spoke to the doctor,' said Fazio, speaking Italian. 'Cosulich is well enough to hear the news.'

He looked at his boss and then said, in a neutral voice: 'If you want to stay here, I can go by myself.'

It would have been one final act of cowardice. 'No, I'll come with you.'

They didn't open their mouths the whole journey. Fazio asked for the room number and then led the way for the inspector, who was walking like an automaton.

Fazio opened the door to the room and went inside. Montalbano waited outside in the hallway.

'Miss Cosulich,' said Fazio.

Montalbano counted to three, summoned his strength, and went in as well.

The head of the bed was slightly raised.

Angelica was wearing an oxygen mask and looking at Fazio.

But as soon as she saw Montalbano come in, she smiled.

The room brightened.

The inspector closed his eyes and kept them closed. 'Angelica Cosulich, I am placing you under arrest,' he heard Fazio say.

Then he turned his back and ran out of the hospital.

Author's Note

Not too long ago in Rome a gang of burglars robbed numerous apartments using the technique described in this novel.

All the rest – the names of people and institutions, events, situations, places, and everything else – was entirely invented by me and has no connection to reality.

Assuming of course that one can exclude reality from a novel.

☆

Angelica's Smile is the first novel I've published with Sellerio since the death of my friend Elvira Sellerio, the founder and publisher of that imprint.

After reading the typescript of the text, Elvira phoned me to point out a huge mistake that had escaped every phase of proofreading and revision by myself and others.

I mention this here just to let you know and remind myself of the care, attention, and affection with which Elvira read her authors.

Notes

*page 27 – **Carlo V**:* This is of course Charles V (1500–1558), Holy Roman Emperor, King of Spain and King of Italy, known in Italy as Carlo Quinto.

page 41 – **with an Umbertine moustache:** That is, in the style of the first King of Italy after the Unification, Umberto I di Savoia (1844–1900), who wore an enormous handlebar moustache.

page 48 – **the PdL:** This is the Polo della Libertà, the right-wing political coalition initially formed around media magnate Silvio Berlusconi's Forza Italia party in 1994.

page 49 – rosticceria . . . cuddriruni . . . arancini, supplì: A *rosticceria* is a take-away serving mostly roast meats; *cuddriruni* is a Sicilian sort of focaccia, served with a broad variety of toppings; and *arancini* are Sicilian fried rice balls usually with mozzarella, peas, and a *ragù* sauce inside, while *supplì* are Roman rice balls, also with mozzarella and tomato sauce inside. *Arancini* are round in shape, generally larger than *supplì*, and can have a greater variety of stuffings, while *supplì* are ovoid and always have more or less the same ingredients.

page 71 – **all dressed up like a paladin in the puppet theatre**: The traditional Sicilian puppet theatre, often performed by itinerant puppet masters, features principally stories drawn from the chivalric romances of the Middle Ages and the Renaissance, which in Italy were mostly derived from the Carolingian tradition.

page 74 – **Ariosto's *Orlando Furioso***: *Orlando Furioso*, a monumentally long serio-comic romance of principally Carolingian derivation (but with many magical and supernatural devices inspired by the Arthurian tradition), written in ottava rima, was the masterwork of Ludovico Ariosto (1474–1533), a poet of the Duke of Este's court in the northern Italian city of Ferrara. *Orlando Furioso* furnishes many of the chivalric episodes used in the Sicilian puppet theatre.

page 74 – ***This knight . . . held him fast***: Ariosto, *Orlando Furioso*, I, 12. This and the majority of the excerpts from Ariosto in this book are drawn from the masterly Barbara Reynolds translation, first published in 1975 by Penguin Books. All subsequent excerpts are from that edition unless otherwise indicated, and will be documented in these notes only as *OF*, with canto and strophe numbers. In certain cases I had to retranslate the excerpt because the Reynolds translation no longer contained the textual ambiguities that enabled Camilleri to apply the passage to his own story.

NOTES

page 75 – **More than a month . . . satisfied:** *OF*, XIX, 34.

page 75 – **Like milky curds . . . breasts:** *OF*, XI, 68.

page 75 – **Actually, those breasts were not Angelica's:** Indeed they refer instead to Olimpia, another of the love interests in *Orlando Furioso*.

page 78 – *A flood of sorrow . . . checked:* *OF*, XXIII, 113.

page 79 – *He sees . . . a hundred times:* *OF*, XXIII, 103. My translation.

page 80 – *And every time . . . hand:* *OF*, XXX, 111. My translation.

page 80 – *a fisher . . . pearl:* A quote from the poem 'Adolescente' by Vincenzo Cardarelli (1887–1959).

page 81 – *Of all . . . check:* *OF*, XXIII, 121.

page 83 – *I am not . . . to be:* *OF*, XXIII, 128. My translation.

page 87 – *The more . . . pain:* *OF*, XXIII, 117. My translation.

page 94 – *A wound . . . unseen:* *OF*, XIX, 27. My translation.

page 97 – *She felt . . . encompassed it:* *OF*, XIX, 26.

page 99 – *For love . . . this breeze:* *OF*, XIII, 127.

page 100 – *Ah, cruel Love! . . . correspond:* *OF*, II, 1.

page 106 – 'Guarda come dondolo': A 1962 pop song by Edoardo Vianello. It means 'See how I sway'.

page 106 – *And thus . . . stone*: OF, I, 39. My translation.

page 107 – *More than an hour*: OF, I, 40. My translation.

page 109 – *With sweet . . . billed*: OF, I, 54.

page 122 – **Gustavo Salvini or Ermete Zacconi**: Salvini (1839–1930) and Zacconi (1857–1948) were celebrated actors of the stage who performed principally in the classical vein.

page 126 – **to say he was sorry to an officer of the carabinieri**: In Italy, the carabinieri are a separate law-enforcement institution and a branch of the army, and are in frequent competition with the civil police bureaucracy of *commissariati* and *questure*, of which Montalbano is part. The carabinieri are also popularly considered to be stupid and are frequently the butt of jokes.

page 131 – *That in this very bed . . . denies*: OF, XXIII, 123.

page 131 – *No less . . . he flies*: OF, XXIII, 123. Adapted from the Barbara Reynolds translation to fit the context.

page 134 – *which no despoiling hand had ever touched*: OF, XIX, 33.

page 169 – *sartù . . . nunnatu*: A Neapolitan rice casserole dish consisting normally of rice, ragù, peas, mushrooms, provolone cheese or *fior di latte* mozzarella, small meatballs, sausages, and chicken livers.

NOTES

page 173 – Not far away . . . gay: OF, I, 37.

page 176 – Son et lumière: A sound and light show invented by Paul Robert-Houdin in 1952 whereby a space, usually a historic monument, is transformed through the use of light and sound.

page 177 – Orlando . . . no more: OF, XXXIX, 61.

*page 195 – **Ugo Foscolo . . . Zakynthos***: Ugo Foscolo (1778–1827), an Italian poet and revolutionary, the son of a Venetian nobleman and a Greek mother, was born on the Greek island of Zakynthos.

*page 204 – **'What's in the basket?' . . . 'Ricotta'***: Sicilian saying, roughly equivalent to 'What's two plus two?' 'Four.'

*page 225 – **The Fable of the Transformed Son***: 'La Favola del Figlio cambiato', a story by Luigi Pirandello (1867–1936).

page 257 – 'Alas! . . . What shall I do? . . .': OF, I, 41.

page 271 – Sitting on a rock . . . would be: OF, X, 34. My translation.

Notes by Stephen Sartarelli